He was out fo
was his bait..

"What sort of
about?" he ask   ...e voice.

"I don't have any future, Mr. Ransome."

He nodded agreement. "You haven't a
chance," he said. "Not the way things are
now. But I can change all that, Melody. I
can help you so easily…"

"BAIT's depiction of an evil womanizer
and his sexually degraded victim is
boldly realistic and uncompromising.
High-octane stuff by a talented
writer."—Bill Pronzini

BAIT
by William Vance
Writing as George Cassidy

Black Gat Books • Eureka California

BAIT

Published by Black Gat Books
A division of Stark House Press
1315 H Street
Eureka, CA 95501, USA
griffinskye3@sbcglobal.net
www.starkhousepress.com

BAIT
Originally published in paperback by Beacon Books as by
"George Cassidy" and copyright © 1962 by Universal
Publishing and Distributing Corporation, New York. York..

ISBN: 979-8-88601-093-0

Cover design by Jeff Vorzimmer, ¡caliente!design, Austin, Texas
Book design by Mark Shepard, shepgraphics.com
Cover art by Jack Faragasso

First Stark House Press/Black Gat Edition: May 2024

ONE

"Aw, come on, Mellie," Kenney said softly.

Melody Frane honestly wanted to please him. But she knew she would not give in. She took Kenney's hand from her warm young breast and said, "Please don't touch me like that." She had to stifle the inner yearning she felt, ignore an impulse to abandon herself and satisfy her own aching want.

She had long ago made a decision based on tough thinking. As a migratory farm worker she could look forward to little, she knew. Her only asset was a body that happened to be beautiful. She was saving that body for a time and place she could not even visualize. And this was not the time, exciting though Kenney might be; further, it was most certainly not the place.

Kenney Ward was the Ransome Company pilot. At the moment, he and Melody happened to be in a two-engine airplane high over the Arizona desert. He had the craft on automatic pilot and they were seated in the wide berth behind the two bucket seats that faced the controls. Odd, to be in the sky with Kenney, the muted roar of the engines in her ears, the sun shining brightly and the blue air all around.

She had been frightened, first of flight itself and more when Kenney had switched on the automatic and motioned her to the rear. But she was no stranger to fear. When Kenney had pinned her to the cushion, crudely trying to pull off her jeans and blouse, she had fought him off and with success. Now he sat pouting sullenly, his hands gripping his knees as though he were nursing his hurt.

"What if we ran into another plane?" she asked.

He made a deprecating gesture. "We're down near the border. Not another aircraft within miles of here."

"What if Mr. Ransome found out?"

The frown grew deeper on Kenney's tanned face. "He doesn't care what I do as long as I'm around when he wants me."

"Maybe he wants you right now."

"What's the matter? Aren't you enjoying yourself?" There was a tinge of bitterness in his voice.

His bitterness bothered her not at all. "Of course I'm enjoying myself. This is my first plane ride."

He looked at her speculatively. "I'd never know it. You haven't lost control for a minute."

"Did you ever really—have—have a girl in this airplane?" she asked.

He laughed. He looked wonderful to her when he laughed. "I'm not saying—but did you ever hear of the mile-high club?"

Melody shook her honey-colored head.

"Maybe I'll tell you some time. What's the pitch? I know you like me. Why so cold?"

A mile high, Kenney said. Melody usually felt humbler. Being up here seemed to release some protest inside her. This was like rising out of a world that had never been gentle with her. She smiled, but her words were not light. "Everyone thinks migratory workers are pushovers. And I guess lots of them are. But not me, Kenney. I know the cards are stacked against me and all I have is myself. This body of mine—if I give it away, I'll have nothing left."

"Some body," Kenney said admiringly.

"It's all I have," she repeated simply. "Much as I'd like to, I'm just not going to let a man love me unless he's ready to put a ring on my finger."

"I wish I were a marrying man," he said wistfully.

"You will be when you find the right girl. Anyway, that's your problem, not mine."

He turned and savagely pulled her close to him. His mouth covered hers. She responded helplessly for a moment, then pushed against him.

Her jeans ripped and she cried out. "Now look what you've done. Do you hate me, Kenney? Why are you so mean?"

"I want you," he stated. "I'm going to have you—"

"Please, Kenney," she breathed. "Please—it would be like stealing. I'm a virgin."

Slowly the passion went out of his face. He stopped touching her and sat still, tense and brooding, the muscle of his jaw twitching. After a while he returned to the pilot's seat and turned off the automatic control. The plane swung in a viciously steep turn.

He looked at her over his shoulder. His scowl, she thought, was for himself, not her. "Damn if I don't believe you," he said grudgingly.

There still was sunlight in the sky but the earth

was darker.

They landed at dusk and taxied up to the hangar. While Kenney tied down the plane, Melody repaired the damage to her jeans as best she could. Dark had come when he helped her into his jeep.

They drove past the long ranchhouse and into the road that led to the migratory workers' camp. He let her out at the gate, gave her a brief good night and drove off.

She stood alone in the warm velvety night and watched the ruby red of the taillights disappearing beyond a rise. Sighing, she went through the noisy sprawling camp until she came to the cabin she shared with her mother.

The cabin was dark. Melody felt a twinge of anxiety. She went inside and turned on the single bulb that dangled in the center of the one-room cabin. The stark light revealed a kerosene stove, a rickety table and an unmade bed. Melody's mother was out somewhere.

She busied herself making supper.

Her mother had not arrived by the time the food was ready. Mellie ate alone and washed the dishes. She turned out the light and undressed in the darkness. Her cot was in a corner opposite the bed. She fell asleep thinking about Kenney and her first airplane ride.

She awoke from dreamlessness to an awareness of some familiar ugly noise inside the cabin. The sound grated in her ears, on her nerves. She huddled in the darkness, listening to the hoarse breathing of her mother and a companion—a man. She was about to spring from the bed when she faced her life's central problem again—where would she go from here? She sank back, listless and unhappy. This pattern was familiar. She tried not to hear the obscene sounds that came from the bed across the room but the effort was like trying not to breathe. Quivering with shame, she listened to her mother's muffled moans interspersed with savage grunts from Joe Priddy and the frantic protests of the rusty bedsprings.

Her revulsion died gradually. She escaped into a memory of Kenney Ward and his strong clean hands touching her in passion. She liked Kenney—maybe too much.

A keening sound came from Effie Frane. "Joe, wait —Joe—"

The crescendo of passion rose to a new high and then stopped suddenly.

Joe Priddy seemed to fall asleep at once.

The woman beside him whimpered, "Come on now, Joe, wake up—I want more—"

Melody pulled the pillow over her head and tried to sleep.

Melody Frane was seventeen that summer. She had a thirty-seven-inch bust, a tiny waist and hips just an inch under her bust measurement. She had lied to Kenney Ward about her virginity, which she had lost at the tender age of eleven. But there had been no one else since that day, down on the edge of the Texas cotton belt, when an itinerant field hand had raped her. She seldom thought about that terrifying incident. Not any more. She worried more about being called Mellie. No one ever called her Melody except Kenney Ward.

The day after her airplane trip was another working day.

Just before noon Melody pushed her shoulders back, straightening, feeling the sharp change of posture as though it were a knife in her muscles. She stretched, stepped away from the grading table and leaned against a stanchion, surveying the huge open shed where Arizona cantaloupe were graded and packed for shipping. The hot spring wind fanned through the packing shed, bringing grit from the desert but no relief from the heat.

Idly, she wished she were rich—more profoundly, she wished she had someone to love her. She looked beyond the desert, where rust-colored mountains rose to a blue Arizona sky. She wished she could walk away from the shed and its smells of ripening melons, women—and men. She wished she could walk through the sand until she reached the mountains, where she could lose herself.

How wonderful it would be, she reflected, never to look at the world again from under the roof of a packing shed.

Someone pinched her painfully. She whirled. Len Knight, the lead man, was leering at her. His large teeth looked yellow and unhealthy.

"Caught you loafin', didn't I?" he witlessly exulted.

Melody felt heat rushing to her face. "Don't you dare," she said in a voice thinned with fury. "Keep your hands off me."

"Aw, hell," Len grunted, his grin fading. "Get back to work, Mellie. We ain't runnin' no guesthouse." He stared at her intently, his eyes peeling off her clothes. "Not even for a good-looker like you."

She had an impulse to spit and curse that surprised her. Restraining herself, she walked angrily, with an exaggerated hip motion, back to the sorting table. Len Knight's low, nasty chuckle followed her.

Soon he was behind her again and standing close. She could feel his body heat and smell his sweat. "Don't know why you're so all-fired stuck up," he said softly. "What you got to be so snotty about?"

Melody said nothing. Her long slender fingers kept deftly sorting the rough-skinned melon. Maybe if she did not answer, he would go away.

"'Fraid maybe your ol' lady's got all the fixings in your family," Len continued. "She's got enough for both o' you—"

Melody went at him. The reference to her mother had snapped her restraint. She forgot everything but her frustration, her hatred of the trap that was her sole heritage ...

She came back to reality slowly. Two women were holding her. There were deep scratches on Len's sallow face. His lip was swollen badly where she had hit him.

He was holding a hand to his scratches and staring stupidly at her.

Oscar, the bald foreman, was running toward them. He spoke sharply to Len. Len stepped down from the shed, walked slowly out of sight.

Oscar took a pad from his shirt pocket, wrote a rapid memo and handed it to Melody.

"Pick up your pay at the office," he said stonily. "Can't have no fightin' around here, Mellie."

"Don't you want to know what happened?" she asked in an unsteady voice.

He looked at her without expression, as though he were judging the quality of a cantaloupe. He shook his bald head. "I got plenty of help," he said, "and too many other worries to take on one more. You've had it, Mellie."

This was the pattern with her, she thought. She walked the length of the shed to the office, exuding a stiff defiance she did not actually feel. Men were always anxious to help her until they discovered she kept her body to herself. Then they wanted nothing to do with her. Sometimes the barrier she had placed around her body seemed to make men hate her. They wanted to hurt her when they found they could not have her.

She crossed the dock and pushed through a door marked OFFICE. She found herself in a small and gloriously air-conditioned anteroom. A tall dark-haired girl rose from a desk, smiling as she came forward.

Silently, Melody gave her the discharge slip.

The girl searched her file for Melody's time card. She wrote out a check, took it into another and larger office. Melody saw a white-haired, well-dressed man at a desk. He signed the check, glanced at Melody through the open doorway. The dark-haired girl left the private office gracefully and brought the check to Melody.

"I hope you enjoyed working with us," she said. "When you come back don't forget to apply here first."

What lovely manners, Melody thought. What a nice place to work ... maybe she too could study shorthand and learn to type and get a secretarial job. Then, instead of moving all the time, she could stay in one place long enough to know nice people.

A fine dream. But impossible.

"Thank you," she said. "You're very kind."

She walked down the highway. The drivers of three cars tried to pick her up before she reached the gravel road that led toward the camp. A familiar sign announced: MIGRATORY WORKERS—REPORT TO STATE EMPLOYMENT OFFICE. A cluster of small shacks huddled beyond the barbed wire fence. The cluster was Camp No. 1, a duplicate of the place she had stayed in last year and the year before.

All the camps were alike. There was always a wash house in the middle of the shacktown that said MEN on one side and WOMEN on the other and that had a single outside spigot where the workers could draw water for drinking and cooking.

Melody walked past the wash house and entered

the first cabin beyond.

Effie Frane was still in bed, nude. Melody let the screen door bang shut. Effie rolled over and glared at her from bloodshot eyes.

"Can't you make a little less noise?" she asked.

Sweat made an outline of her body where she had sprawled on the sheet. It was hard to believe that Effie had once been smart and pretty.

"What're you lookin' at me like that for?" the older woman demanded.

"I'm just looking, Ma," Melody said. She crossed the room to the washstand, poured water into the tin basin and began soaping her hands. She smeared the lather on her face and gently rubbed it in.

"Always fussin'," Effie sneered, sitting up heavily. Melody felt a sense of shame at sight of the bloated figure that matched Effie's debauched face. "Always primpin' and washin'. Maybe you think you're better than anybody else."

"Ma, I got fired today."

The older woman's mouth fell open. "Fired?" she echoed.

"Yes, fired."

"What for?"

"Len pinched me and I let him have it. Oscar fired me."

"Oh, for God's sake," her mother said crossly. "Just like that. Where'd he pinch you—ass or tit?"

Melody stared hard at her mother. "Don't talk like that."

"If you was to talk and act more like me, we'd get along a lot better."

"Maybe I don't want to get along that way."

"Maybe you can just walk out and find us another place to live. You know if we don't work we can't stay here."

"Season's almost over, anyway," Melody said reflectively. "We were planning to go on for potatoes—"

"It's too early for potatoes and too late for lettuce." Effie put her face in her hands and began to sob. "Oh, what'll we do, Mellie?"

"Stop bawling."

Her mother stopped crying and glared. "Don't you get funny with me," she said. "You're under age. I can have you in a reform school before you can say scat."

"I wish you would tell me to scat."

"Don't try me."

"If you send me away," Melody asked serenely, "who'll work for you? Yes, and feed and clothe you and take care of you when you're too drunk to take care of yourself—which is most of the time?"

"Lot you care," Effie Frane moaned, swaying to and fro. She paused, asked again, "What're we gonna do?"

"I don't know," Melody said. "I'll think about it."

"Think, think, think," shouted Effie Frane, her breasts flopping with the violence of her motions. She put her hands over them and slid out of bed. Her distended belly was blue-veined and blotched.

Melody turned away, sickened, looking at the wall rather than at her mother.

"Put your clothes on, Ma. I'll go buy something for lunch."

"That's right. Go into town." Effie's voice was suddenly wheedling. "I need—"

"You don't need a drink, Ma." Melody said. She hung up her towel and left the shack with her mother's cruses in her ears.

TWO

Joe Priddy was standing outside, a sly grin on his dark face. Melody smelled him when she stopped. He stank of sweat and drink, and somehow also of her mother's bed the night before.

He asked, "Effie home?"

Mellie nodded and started to move on.

He stepped in front of her. "What's the big rush?"

"I'm going to the store."

"Heard you got canned."

"You heard right."

"What you gonna do now?"

"Haven't decided." She changed direction but again Priddy stepped in front of her. "Get out of my way, Joe," she told him softly.

"Oh, I ain't gonna hurt you none."

"You're right there."

"Smart little bitch, ain't you?" Priddy growled, his grin fading. "What you so damn stuck up about? You're made just like all the girls I know."

Her heart pounded and she felt her temper rising. "Joe, leave me alone."

"Or what?"

"Or I might claw your eyes out."

He backed away a step. "Hell," he said.

"Joe?" Effie called from inside the shack. "That you out there, Joe?"

"Leave her alone," Melody ordered, but the order carried no weight. She ran up the sandy road as fast as she could. She had to restrain herself to keep from crying. Her tears were the hot tears of rage. No one could make her cry, she told herself. She felt sick inside, knowing Joe Priddy would not leave Effie alone. He could get whatever he wanted from Effie for the price of a drink of whisky.

Melody passed the company store. The migratory workers were hanging around outside. She was conscious of their stares. She passed them without speaking, her feet scuffing sand, and left camp by the gate. The unpaved sand and gravel road reminded her of all the roads she had known from Texas to Washington. Through her life there had been a caravan of junk cars, of lean days when she had no work, and slightly better days when she at least had enough to eat. The cabins, the shacks—or sometimes just a tent beside the highway—these had been home.

She looked up at the sky. The same sky, she thought, that covered people with homes. They breathed the same air, and marveled at the same sunlight. Why was her life so different from theirs in every other way?

A car stopped beside her. Melody Frane kept walking. This, too, was part of all roads she walked on. There were always the men. Young, middle-aged or old, they all wanted her. But Melody Frane herself was not what they wanted. They wanted her body and to hell with Melody afterward.

"Mellie."

The voice was familiar. She stopped and turned.

Oscar Land, the Ransome foreman, opened his car door for her. "The boss wants to see you," he said.

"Sure. So do Dick Clark and Fabian."

"Quit kidding. The boss means business." Oscar looked disturbed.

"What does he want?"

"How should I know? Come on and ask him yourself."

"Tell him you tried, Oscar." Melody kept walking. Oscar drove slowly beside her, sweat beading his bald head.

"Listen, Mellie, the boss don't like it when I don't do what he tells me. Please, honey, come on. He ain't gonna hurt you."

Melody made no comment.

"Mellie, please. Maybe he—he sure got mad because I canned you. You might cost me my job. I got a wife and five lads, Mellie. Please get in the car and let me drive you to the boss' house."

Melody stopped and turned. "You want me to go to his house?"

"That's what he said."

Right now, Melody considered, a boss was what she needed. A boss—a job. She bargained. "You'll wait for me? So you can drive me into town after I've talked to him?"

"Sure, I'll wait."

She climbed in beside him and settled back. The car had a leathery smell of newness. The seat was comfortable, even luxurious. Melody sighed aloud. The car had air conditioning. Foremen must make good money, she thought. More important, they made money regularly. Joe Priddy sometimes made a hundred dollars a day but there were weeks on end when he did not work. A regular paycheck was the main thing.

"Here we are." Oscar's breath expelled gustily. He leaned across Melody to open the car door on her side. In front of them stood a modern rambling ranchhouse, made of adobe. Beyond, there was the desert. Vines on a trellis shaded the porch. A long low foreign car stood in the nearby carport. Beside the smaller car was a Cadillac convertible.

An airstrip adjoined the house, complete with aluminum-colored hangar and two-engine airplane. A man in a floppy straw cowboy hat was working on the airplane. The man was Kenney Ward.

The airplane was the one she had been in yesterday —her first flight.

"Gee, it's nice," Melody said breathlessly.

"Yeah. The boss is rich. Go on in, he's expecting you."

"You'll wait for me?" she asked worriedly. The

sunlight here seemed brighter—almost too bright, she thought.

"Yeah, I'll wait. Now hurry."

She walked up to the door and pushed a button. A small Mexican in a short white jacket opened the door. He smiled at her. "Miss Melody?"

"Yes," she said, pleased that her name was known.

"Right this way, señorita."

She followed him through a cool air-conditioned room and down a carpeted hallway. They passed through wide doors into a sunny study.

A white-haired bronze-faced man rose from an uncluttered desk. He was taller than Melody had expected.

The houseboy left Melody alone with his employer. In spite of the white hair, the man's face was youthful and unlined. He had light blue eyes that reminded her of two marbles embedded in bronze.

"I'm Harry Ransome," he said. The name echoed for Melody. This was the boss, the owner of the Ransome Packing Company. "Sit down." He took her by the arm with hard fingers and led her to a couch that looked upholstered in rawhide.

There were Navajo rugs on the floor and on the wall. Between the rugs on the wall, bookshelves hung. Melody sat. She found the leather couch soft and comfortable.

Ransome leaned against his desk, in khaki trousers, stiff with starch, scuffed cowboy boots and tailored checked shirt that showed off his shoulders and muscles. He was smiling at her.

"I've been watching you," he said.

She drew a breath. The boss. Those were big words. "Why?"

"You're about the prettiest girl I've seen around these parts. How old are you, Melody?"

"Seven—nineteen."

"You mean seventeen, don't you?" He stared hard, the blue eyes still cold as an iceberg.

She found she could not lie to him. "All right," she said defiantly. "I'm seventeen, so what?"

"Why did you lie about your age?"

"It might make a difference to some people."

"You're honest," he said. "I saw that little byplay this morning between you and Len Knight."

"I didn't know you were there."

"That's because I make it a point not to be seen. I didn't discharge Len." He sounded apologetic, which seemed incongruous in so strong a man. "Len's a half-wit but a good worker. I told Oscar I wanted to see you because—" his eyes slitted, studying her— "because I wanted to get to know you better."

She felt her heart quicken. Was this the old familiar pattern? The only difference was the approach and the man making it. Most of the men who wanted her were migratory workers with little subtlety in their make-up.

"How about it, Mellie—me and you?" That was the way they did it and she knew how to deal with them.

This was different. She felt uncomfortable.

"Why should you want to know me?" she asked.

He laughed delightedly. "As I said, I've watched you. I'm attracted to cold women, Melody. Especially if they are beautiful. It's that simple." He was laughing, silently now, his blue eyes almost closed, the wrinkles at the side of his eyes erasing the white lines.

His silent laughter broke into sound. "You're a direct woman, Melody. But you're cold, cold, cold."

Secretly, she felt pleased that this mature man called her a woman. But there was a confidence about him that put her on the defensive almost automatically. "How do you know I'm a cold woman?"

"I've seen every man working for me, from Oscar on down, making a play for you. They had no luck. You went with Kenney for an airplane ride. He usually gets them there. I know for sure he got nowhere with you, Melody."

"He told you that? Kenney Ward?" She felt betrayed.

Mr. Ransome nodded, smiling. "My pilot Kenney Ward."

Melody rose. "Really, Mr. Ransome. I'm just not interested in what you have to say."

His blue eyes seemed to grow darker and he straightened. "Hear me out," he told her quietly. "I'm not propositioning you—not now at least. I want to give you a job, Melody."

"What sort of job?" Her palms felt sweaty and her heart beat even faster. Grudgingly, she admitted to herself that this man had a kind of magnetism. She found herself wanting to do what he wanted her to do. That, she knew, could be dangerous to a girl in her special spot.

"A good job, Melody. My—my secretary up and got married recently. I have to replace her. How'd you like her job?"

She hardened her heart against the persuasion in his voice. "Secretary, Mr. Ransome?" She giggled. "I can't type, can't take shorthand, and I know nothing about filing. Otherwise, I'm perfect for the job."

"That's right," he interrupted, waving his hands. "I'll see that you acquire any skills you need. I'll send you to school—"

She interrupted in turn. "I didn't even finish grammar school," she said. "Please, Mr. Ransome, don't tease me like this. I'm pretty, I know. But I also know there are lots of pretty girls."

Harry Ransome put his hands on her shoulders. He sat down facing her on the couch.

"What sort of future have you thought about?" he asked in a gentle voice.

She was aware of a choking sensation in her throat. What sort of future had she thought about? She had not dared even to dream about anything really triumphant. And right now, all she could think about was the bleak reality that probably lay ahead. "I don't have any future, Mr. Ransome."

Unsmiling, he nodded agreement. "You haven't a chance," he said. "Not the way things are now. But I can change all that, Melody. The biggest bar to your success, your happiness and eventual fulfillment is a lack of education. Seems a shame—when I can help you so easily."

She thought of her mother and shuddered.

Suddenly she sensed the dynamic tension that was latent in the man. The tension imparted itself to her. He stood for something for which Melody felt awe— and he had sent for her, singled her out. She could handle men like Joe Priddy, whom she understood and despised. Harry Ransome was different. She lay back against the couch, looking into his face, her lips parted.

He did not speak. Part of Melody protested as his fingers plucked at her clothing, but the protest was silent and inward. Had he asked permission, spoken any word whatever, she could have denied him. But he took her in lordly manner, as though she were his by right. She felt the weight of him, half-startled, half-shamed by her own thrill of pleasure. The man made love with a kind of tempered violence, as though this were an introduction.

Then they were apart. Ransome sat at her feet, his head on the back of the couch, his eyes closed.

The door of the study flew open. Effie Frane came charging into the room.

Melody scrambled to her feet, grabbed her jeans and began slipping into them. Joe Priddy stood behind Melody's obese mother. He was grinning. Somehow, Melody thought dazedly, the pair had sneaked past the houseboy.

Ransome reached casually for one of the Navajo

rugs and draped it over his lap.

"My little girl, my little girl," Effie screeched in a voice of doom.

Joe Priddy patted the fat shoulder. "Tell 'im," he said snugly. "Gonna cost you plenty, Mr. Rich Man. That gal's under age." He leered. "San Quentin quail it's known as." He threw back his head and laughed.

THREE

Joe Priddy wilted under Ransome's steady stare. Draped in a Navajo rug, a lesser man would have appeared ludicrous. But the tall rancher still commanded respect. "Sanchez?" he snapped in a carrying voice. An instant later, the houseboy came into the study.

"Sanchez, take these people out to the patio," Ransome ordered. "Give them a drink. I'll join you shortly."

When Joe and Effie were herded away, Melody said, "Gee, I hope they don't cause you any trouble, Mr. Ransome."

He smiled. "My name is Harry. Run into the powder room and tidy up. They won't cause any trouble. Don't worry about it, Melody."

As she turned obediently away, he leaned down and kissed her lightly.

"Were going to get along fine," he said.

The powder room, evidently for the use of female

guests, was exquisite and small, decorated in shades of turquoise and silver. Melody forgot to hurry, as she lingered in admiration, until she heard a tap on the door, and her host's amused voice. "When you're ready, come out to the patio, Melody."

He had known she would be impressed. Flustered, she dressed hurriedly. In this place, her jeans seemed cruder and rougher than ever. Queer—at a time like this to be ashamed of your clothing—instead of feeling shame for what you had done, if you were Melody Frane. But in this house Ransome was law—and she had obeyed the law.

She found the patio. Priddy and her mother sat there gulping tall drinks. Melody watched Ransome talking to them as though a couple of field hands invaded his privacy every day. Melody was appalled to see that Effie had crossed her legs and raised her skirt indecently. She walked determinedly over to her mother.

"You don't have a thing to worry about, Mr. Ransome," she said in a steely voice. "Ma and me are going right now. We're not going to bother you."

"You're out of your mind," Effie shrilled. "You can't tell me what to do. I'm your mother."

"My God, don't I know it," Melody agreed from the depths of her being.

Joe Priddy put in piously, "Better listen to your ma."

"You shut up, Joe Priddy," Melody told him.

"There's no need for anyone to get excited," Ransome said. He was trying not to laugh, Melody realized.

"You're not going to get away with this." Effie meant to cling to that. She finished her drink with a single gulp, put down her glass, and stood up. "Come on, Joe, we're going to town and tell the police. That'll fix him."

"Wait a minute, Effie," Joe Priddy said uneasily. "Maybe you don't have to do anything like that." His voice took on a servile note. "Mr. Ransome looks to me like a mighty fine man."

"Ma, you and Joe come right along this minute," Melody begged. Without waiting to see if they would obey, she darted away. Harry Ransome's quick hard tone faded in her hearing.

She had all but forgotten Oscar, but realized as she left the house that he was not waiting for her as he had promised he would do. She was not too accustomed to people keeping their promises to her, anyway.

She walked down the driveway and into the road, thinking about Ransome's caresses and lovemaking. He had awed her—but he had not fulfilled her. She was still stirred and restless.

She looked across the flight strip and saw Kenney wiping his hands on a rag, obviously just finishing a chore with the plane. She climbed the fence and joined him.

Surprise and pleasure washed over his brown face.

"Hi, kid," he said. "How's it going?"

"Fine."

"What're you doing way out here?"

"I dunno. Just walking."

"Well, come on over and I'll get you a can of beer out of the icebox."

"I don't like beer."

"Maybe I can find a coke or something." He swung away and she followed him, noting the wide spread of his shoulders and the slenderness of his hips in the faded skin-tight jeans. The floppy straw cowboy hat that he wore even when flying seemed peculiarly his.

He opened a small door in the hangar, held it for her. Inside, the hot dimness smelled of gas and oil and engines. A corner was partitioned off by a straw curtain. Kenney went behind the curtain and came out with a can of beer and a bottle of Seven-Up. They took their drinks outside to the shade of the hangar.

Kenney motioned Melody into a metal lounge chair. She sank into the chair, gratefully lifting her feet, and sipped the drink.

"Mr. Ransome wants me to work for him," she said.

"But you already work for him." He stared at her and she noticed that his eyes were not always brown. Right now, for instance, they were a coppery color, almost the shade of his hair.

"He wants me to be his private secretary," she said. "He'll send me to school so I can learn all I have to know."

"Don't do it."

"Why do you say that?"

He lowered the beer can and wiped his mouth with the back of his hand. "Look, Melody honey, you're a real sweet girl. And a virgin—you told me so. He's twice as old as you."

She was suddenly frightened because of what had happened in Harry Ransome's study. Had she turned into a different kind of girl? All she said was, "What's that got to do with me working for him?"

"You work for him, first thing he'll do is have you in bed."

"I can take care of myself," she protested unhappily, already knowing that she could not take care of herself with Harry Ransome.

"Not with this cookie. He'd have you before you knew it. He's slick, honey."

"Don't you like him?"

"Sure I like him, but he's a dog. He's given away a dozen convertibles since I started working for him two years ago."

"Given away convertibles—you mean cars?"

"Sure, cars. He has himself a girl, usually a young one—he's crazy about young females—and they squawk and he gives 'em a car. That pays up, see?"

"He looks awfully nice."

"Yeah. But he's not half as nice as he looks. He's a mean sonofabitch, Melody."

"I thought you said you liked him."

"I do." He frowned at her. "But some of the things he does I don't like. Get it?"

"No. What does he do you don't like?"

"I'd hate to say, Melody. I can't prove it."

"Tell me, Kenney. I won't tell anyone else."

"He's rich, you know that. He owns the airplane I

fly but that's peanuts. The seven-fifty a month that he pays me is peanuts. He owns more than lettuce fields and cantaloupe patches. The packing shed and all that goes with it is just a fraction. He also owns an electronic plant in Tucson, a television station or two, and part of a Vegas hotel."

"What's wrong with being rich?"

"Nothing, nothing at all. But to stay rich or get richer, he has to be a mean sonofabitch like I said. He gets people to do what he wants by blackmailing them."

"He wouldn't," Melody stated.

"I know he does," Kenney said doggedly. "Don't have anything to do with him, Melody. He'll hurt you."

"I wasn't planning on being hurt," she said, rising and smiling at him. "Thanks for the drink, Kenney."

"Stick around and I'll make us a hamburger." The sun was dropping behind the mountains. The sky was a riot of color, the mountains mysteriously purple. Did the sky and mountains also belong to Ransome? Well, in a way they did. Suddenly she felt a reckless fervor seething within her, an eagerness to plunge headlong into Harry Ransome's wonderful world.

Yet intuition told her Kenney was right about the older man. She said, "All right, Kenney. A hamburger —but nothing else."

He set his beer can aside, leaned toward her and looked into her eyes. He said, "I'm just of a darn good mind to become a marrying man, Melody."

"Don't do anything you'd be sorry for."

"I'm never sorry." He kissed her lips.

Longing coursed through her, as though the kiss had been a farewell. "We'll be moving on," she whispered. "We'll leave here soon, Kenney, and I'll never see you again."

"You won't leave me," he said. "You only have shoes, Melody. And I have wings. I won't let you get away."

They clung to one another. In her restlessness and uncertainty, she felt that Kenney was all the answers, however briefly, to all the world's troubling questions. She cradled herself against him and a warm wind caressed their bodies. She touched him with her hands and with her mouth and his demanding body covered hers, hard and buffeting, assaulting her with a furious intensity that set them both aflame. She felt as though no man had ever had her before. Not like this.

The man she had been with only a little while ago, the imperious man who had aroused in her something that was only half desire, another half docile submission to his authority—he did not count, she told herself. Harry Ransome might own a large fraction of Arizona as well as points east and west, but he was nowhere near the man Kenney was.

Harry had left her largely untouched. He had merely aroused her, made her want to be loved.

But she had risen from Harry's conquest of her— she realized she had been a conquest, nothing more —feeling restless, erotically unfulfilled. Feeling alone, as though she had not been close to anyone at all.

She and Kenney parted—and loved again. Every fibre of her body exulted in their reunion. She was tireless, she found. The years of hard outdoor work, she had always sensed, would either kill her early or strengthen her beyond average endurance.

Kenney had a strength to match her own.

He made her want him just by touching her, just by grazing his hard legs across her own trembling ones. Her desire was as immediate as fire, a rage of love and need—and he satisfied that rage, beating his own need into her aching softness with a rhythm new to her, a rhythm that seemed just and true as the rhythm of seasons or coursing stars—

If only this never would end, this falling, rising, reaching—this ecstasy that could not expand and which nevertheless expanded until she felt she must burst with fulfillment—

Kenney, Kenney, Kenney—

If only Ransome had not had her. If only—

At last they paused and Kenney lay beside her in the shade, holding her blond head in the crook of his arm. He said softly, "I'm way up on a mountain, Melody honey. Nobody there but you and me."

"Sure," she said dreamily.

"You've got to belong to me, Melody. I don't want another woman, not ever. Just you." He kissed her ear.

"Hush, now."

"I mean it." He sat up suddenly, looking at her with that coppery glint in his eyes. "I love you, Melody girl. I want you for my wife."

She started to laugh hysterically, but stopped herself.

If only he had asked her an hour ago—

"Damn it," he shouted in hurt. "What's so funny?"

She put her hand on his deep muscular chest that was covered with small fine hair. "I'm sorry, Kenney. But—"

"But what? I ask you to marry me and you laugh. I take it back, Melody."

"I'm sorry if I hurt your feelings." She got off the sun chair and straightened her shirt and jeans. "I didn't mean to."

He went into the hangar and came out carrying a small grill. She watched him build a fire with charcoal briquettes. Two hamburger patties and matching buns seemed to require his full attention. He soon had a good smell coming from the small grill. He never once looked at her and the frown did not leave his face.

"I said I was sorry," she said hesitantly.

"Forget it. I didn't mean it, anyway."

"Now you're trying to hurt me. I don't blame you." Finally he turned his back on the grill and took her hands in his. "Damn it, Melody, having you was like nothing I've ever had before. I've slept with a lot of women but you're the most. You've got to be mine, all mine. There's just one way it's done."

"I'm just seventeen," she said.

He groaned remorsefully. "But I didn't know, honey. Now you've got to marry me."

"Why?" she asked wonderingly.

"Because they could put me in jail. You know that as well as I do."

"I won't tell anyone. Anyway, I can pass for twenty-one."

"I'm asking you just once more, Melody. Will you marry me?"

She stroked his hair as he knelt beside her chair. "I'd like to," she said softly, "but it won't work, Kenney. In a little while, when the new all wore off, you'd wonder about me."

"What do you mean, wonder?" he asked roughly.

"Well, you'd think—she did it with me before we were married. Maybe she's done it with someone else ... things like that."

"No I wouldn't," he said fiercely.

"That's what you say now." She kissed him. His mouth was unyielding. "You're real sweet, Kenney, a really swell guy. That's why I'm saying no."

He rose slowly and went back to the grill. He huddled over it and turned the hamburgers, his broad shoulders bent. She felt sorry for him, so sorry that she was tempted to tell him she would marry him. Life could be good, she thought, if she were married to a man like Kenney, a real man, with power and drive and a profession. She would enjoy not having to travel from one migratory camp to another. But she knew it would not work out. She remained silent, watching him with a growing ache inside her.

He brought her one of the hamburgers and another Seven-Up. They ate in silence. When they finished eating, the sun was low. He dumped the coals from the grill, scraped sand over them and put the grill away.

"Come on," he said unhappily. "I'll drive you home."

She went with him wordlessly, walking behind him, climbing into the jeep beside him. He started the engine and spun the wheels as they rocketed away from the hangar. She looked toward the ranch house. Several cars were parked in the driveway.

"Must be having a party up there," she said lightly.

"Ransome has a party every night." Kenney raced the jeep down the road, careened into the work camp and came to a wheel-sliding stop in front of her cabin. "See you, Melody," he said shortly.

"Aren't you going to kiss me goodbye?" she asked, leaning toward him.

He kissed her hard, savagely, with a bitter intimation of passion.

She drew away from him.

"Don't let me keep you," he said. When she left the jeep he gunned the motor and raced away, raising a cloud of dust. She watched him until he went through the gate, and then, sighing, she turned into the shack.

She switched on the single light bulb and stared emptily. Joe Priddy and her mother lay on Effie's bed in a drunken stupor. They were both half-dressed. Empty bottles littered the floor beside them.

Where did they get all the liquor? Melody wondered how they could pay for it.

She stood for a full minute staring at the scene, her heart cold inside her. Then she went to her corner and pulled out a battered suitcase from under her cot. She hurriedly packed her few belongings and snapped the lid. On a piece of paper torn from an empty sack, she scribbled a hasty message.

> Dear Ma: I'm going away for good.
> Don't try to find me, please.

She signed her name and set the note on a window ledge above the water bucket, where her mother would be sure to find it.

She picked up her suitcase, switched off the light and closed the door behind her. Above her the sky showed the first star. She breathed deeply—a breath of relief. She walked down the road, past the gate, and into the highway. She headed toward Harry Ransome's house.

Whatever Ransome had to offer could not be worse than the life she already knew.

FOUR

When Melody reached the big ranchhouse, dark had come. The house was ablaze with lights. She picked her way through the cluster of parked cars. Music and laughter came from behind the drawn drapes. She pressed the doorbell button for the second time that day.

After a long wait, while she tried to decide whether to ring again, or simply run off to nowhere, the door opened. Sanchez peered out.

"Miss Melody," he said, surprised. "I don't theenk Mr. Ransome is expecting you. He didn't—"

"I know, I know," Melody said nervously. She was still almost of a mind to make up any excuse and dart away. The sickening memory of her mother held her to her original resolution. "He isn't expecting me, Sanchez. But I would like to see him for just a minute."

Sanchez hesitated. "You go in the study, please. I'll see if he can come." The houseboy opened the door wide.

Melody could see that Sanchez meant to be kind. In her distracted state, the kindness calmed her disproportionately. There are nice people in the world, she thought. She went down the hallway, feeling an instant pleasure in the air-conditioning after the outside heat.

She caught a glimpse of Harry Ransome's guests through the wide doors that opened into the living room.

A group of men stood at the picture window that looked out on the desert. Were they really enjoying themselves as much as they seemed to be doing? Drinks in hand, they were laughing, talking, smoking, seemingly with great amiability. Some women sat on the floor in a semicircle. They were holding drinks, too, and smoking and laughing and carrying on. They looked drunk to Melody, but no one paid any attention to them. Women had no business drinking, she thought. They lost all womanliness when they got soused. If they only knew how they looked to other people. She hurried on to the study.

The room, though she remembered it in clear detail, seemed different now. The change, she thought, was in herself. What had happened here earlier today seemed remote and unreal. She was not the same girl who had given herself to Harry Ransome on that rawhide couch. She did not know what the changes were, only that they had occurred.

She turned as Ransome came into the study.

"I'm sorry," she said. "Busting in like this on your party."

"Never mind that," he said with a broad, reassuring smile. "Melody, is anything wrong?"

"Ma—my mother—" Melody felt her eyes grow warm and moist. "I don't know if I can tell you—"

He led her to the couch gently, made her sit. "You can talk to me, Melody. I'm your friend."

"You don't mind me coming here like this?"

"Mind? I'm delighted."

"What I really wanted to tell you," Melody said in a low voice, "was that I—" She stopped speaking as a slim, dark-haired woman came into the room. Melody had seen her a moment before, sitting on the floor and laughing with the other women. She was simply and strikingly dressed in a silk sheath the color of coffee—without cream.

"What is it this time, Harry?" she asked, taking in Melody with a single sharp glance. "Couldn't it wait until tomorrow?"

Ransome rose and said politely, "Hope, this is Melody Frane. She's going to take Josie's place. Melody, this is Mrs. Ransome."

"How nice," Mrs. Ransome said without warmth. "I didn't think anyone could take Josie's place, Harry."

Ransome studied his wife with ice-blue eyes. "I think she'll be much better than Josie," he said.

Hope Ransome compressed her lips and left the room without having acknowledged her introduction to Melody.

Melody looked at the closed door then turned to her host.

"I didn't know—you were married," she said in a low voice. She supposed she was reaching frantically for excuses. She might have said other things. I didn't know I was cheating a strange woman, as well as a strange man. Two cheated people—your wife and the man who might some day have been my husband ...

Ransome laughed a thin laugh. "Don't let it bother you." He added in a normal voice, "I'm really glad you've made your mind up, Melody."

Apparently, he had guessed she was ready to take him up on his offer of a job. "Yes," she said dully. "I've made up my mind, I guess. I'll start any time—I'm free now, Mr. Ransome."

"Would you care to join the party?"

"Join the party?" Melody was startled. "I'm not dressed for a party. And, anyway, I don't think I'd feel —feel—"

"Welcome?"

"That's it," she agreed, feeling warm in spite of the air-conditioning.

"Nonsense. But I know you must be tired. I'll have Sanchez drive you back to the camp."

"I'm not going there any more. Not ever."

He seemed to understand instantly. "To a motel, then. I'll see you tomorrow."

"I can manage all right by myself."

He put his arm around her slim waist, resting a hand on the plenteous mound of her breast. "But I've a personal interest in you now, Melody. I don't want you out alone at night."

"Whatever you say." She felt his hand dropping possessively to the curve of her hip. She thought of Kenney—a lost, sad, lonely thought.

Ransome's hand tightened its grip briefly. He caressed her neck with his lips. "That's the stuff," he pronounced with satisfaction. "We're going to have a lot of fun together, Melody."

"Fun?"

"Work should be fun," he told her. "I'll make arrangements tomorrow to start your job training. After that—" He shrugged. "Melody, how would you like to travel?"

"Travel?"

"What you need is schooling—more than you'd get around here. I'll have to send you away for a little while. You'll be leaving in less than a week. Meanwhile, be my guest—here, at a motel, wherever you're more comfortable. Will that be all right?"

"Yes," she said tiredly. All Melody had was shoes, Kenney Ward had told her—Kenney himself had wings.

Wings that could follow where Harry Ransome sent her?

FIVE

Two mornings later, Melody awoke and stretched luxuriously. Somewhere out of sight, an air-conditioning unit hummed softly, comfortingly. The blazing Arizona sun defied the drapery at the windows of her sleeping chamber. The motel room was light.

Melody sat up in bed, the covers dropping away from her smooth shoulders. She hugged her long, slim legs, looking at herself in the full length mirror on the bathroom door.

She had never dreamed that a motel could be as grand as this. Soft beige carpeting covered the floor. The furniture was attractive and new and polished. There were prints on the wall. Not a speck of dust showed anywhere.

She watched herself get out of bed and pirouetted in front of the mirror, laughing when her foot caught on the trailing bedclothes. She turned on the shower in the bathroom. Just one little old handle and the water was hot immediately, no waiting. She closed the glass door of the shower stall and reveled in her ablutions.

She was toweling off when someone tapped on the door. Hastily she wrapped the towel around herself and walked to the door. "Who is it?" she asked.

"It's me—Kenney."

His voice sounded angry.

"What do you want?" she called, suddenly no longer pleased with herself.

"I'm supposed to fly you down to Los Angeles," he said, still in that hard, angry voice. "But I want to talk to you first."

"I'm not dressed."

"Well, cover yourself and let me in. I can't stand out here shouting at you."

She pinned the towel in place around herself and opened the door. He walked into the room, shut the door behind him, and looked unhappily down at her. Finally he said, "You can't do it, Melody. You can't get mixed up with Ransome. I won't let you."

"Please," she said in a small voice. "I have to do what I have to do."

Again, he seemed at a loss for words. Then, with a kind of sob, he scooped her up in his arms and the towel slipped away.

He kissed her smooth white stomach, kneeling in front of her, his arms locked about her legs, as though she were some idol to whom he desperately turned.

She gasped, terrified by the tenderness she felt. She stroked his hair, whispered his name.

He came to his feet and lifted her in his arms. He moved toward the bed.

They lay side by side where she had slept alone. She felt the hardness of him as her fingers roved over his muscular arm. He covered her mouth with his and they melted together. Kenney's hoarse breathing mingled with her soft moans of pleasure. "Darling," she heard herself say to him. "Darling, I love you, love you—"

A curious thing happened, perhaps from the sheer intensity of their lovemaking, perhaps because of its hopelessness.

She loved Kenney—and she might lose him because of what had happened between her and Ransome. Her head felt light. The room and all its luxury, which Harry Ransome had provided, seemed to fade away as she lay in Kenney's arms. She came back to awareness to find Kenney looking at her in wonderment and alarm, his cheek against his palm, his elbow on the pillow. She smiled at him, opening her eyes wide, and pulled him to her.

"I'm all right," she said. "I guess I'm just not used to this much happiness."

With the first crazy heat of passion gone, he made love to her again gently, tenderly—this was beautiful and new, as though before this moment no man and woman had ever loved.

He kissed her ear and said, "This is marriage, Melody —in all but the name."

"Please don't say that."

"I'll ask you over and over. I love you, Melody. Don't you understand that I want you to be my wife, not my mistress? I want you all for myself, all the time, forever."

"I want to belong to you too, Kenney. It can't work out. I'm not good enough, or smart enough, or strong enough—"

"And I'm not rich enough," he ended the moment harshly. "But you go along with what Ransome wants and you'll wind up sad and lonely. I'm telling you." He rose from the bed and added grimly, "All right, Melody. Now you can get dressed." He left her.

She did not look at the mirror as she walked into the bathroom to shower again and to dress.

She admitted to herself that she was more than a little scared. She wished she had someone to talk to, someone smarter than she was, who would listen to her and care about what was happening to her and give her good advice.

She had always wanted to get the good things of life for herself, but there was one thing she could never have, no matter how lucky she was—and that was a mother who would want her to be happy, who would listen.

Right now she needed someone like that.

She tried to be her own mother, playing a sad little game with herself in which she told herself her problems and tried to find the answers.

I love Kenney Ward, Melody said silently to the mother who was not there. When I saw love in the movies when I was a kid, I didn't know what the excitement was all about. I thought love was just the opposite of what Ma does with Joe Priddy. I thought love was the things that someone like Harry Ransome can give a girl. Nobody told me love would make you want to give instead of take.

Nobody told you the make-believe silent voice of the nonexistent mother echoed in her thoughts.

Maybe a person like Melody wasn't entitled to love.

The make-believe adviser in Melody's brain began subtly to obey Melody, to agree with every suggestion Melody made.

Everything would be all right, the voice assured Melody. All Melody had to do from now on was watch her step with Harry Ransome, remember that he had hired her for a secretarial job, for which he would have her trained. She would keep Harry in his place. She would work for him, that was all.

The love between her and Kenney had nothing to do with Harry.

She must make Kenney see that. Right now he saw Harry Ransome as a threat to his love for Melody.

She knew in her heart that the threat was real. She made believe she was not afraid.

Kenney was quiet on the flight down to Los Angeles. He spoke to Melody just once, during the trip, to ask if she was cold. He adjusted the heat when she gave an affirmative answer.

Not before the city was spread out there before them did he turn his coppery head to look at her for more than a brief instant. "I'm not going to ask you now," he said, his brown throat working, "but I'm not forgetting you, Melody. No matter what happens, I'll be around."

She felt frightened by the words, relieved to have him speak to her. "What can happen?"

He shrugged. "Forget it. Nothing will happen."

"But you meant something."

"Skip it."

"I'm just going to take a business course. That's all."

He smiled joylessly. "We'll see." He turned from her, and busied himself with calling the airport tower for permission to land.

He landed the plane smoothly, taxied to the main building and shut off the engine. A few minutes later, Melody heard him tell the attendant that he would be leaving shortly and that he needed only gas and oil. She felt a vague panic at the thought of his leaving her in the city. But he was still with her at the information booth where a tall, middle-aged woman seemed to be waiting for them.

"Mrs. Matthews, this is Melody Frane," Kenney said. "Melody, Linda Matthews."

Mrs. Matthews was dark-haired, dark-eyed and, Melody thought, beautiful. She took Melody's hand and said, "What a lovely child," in a deep husky voice.

"Yeah," Kenney said. "Well, I got to get back to the ranch."

"Thanks so much for bringing her," Mrs. Matthews said. Her dark eyes greedily fastened on Kenney's muscular body, and she looked suddenly less beautiful.

"I wish you could stay longer some time, Kenneth."

"Yeah. Well. You know the boss."

"Yes," Linda Matthews said. "I know the boss. We all work for him, don't we?"

"Yeah. Well, so long."

Melody watched him walk away, her throat swelling until she felt she would suffocate. She wanted to run after him and beg him to take her with him. She bit her lip to repress the call that threatened to burst from her lips.

"Come along, dear," Linda Matthews said.

"Can—can I wait and watch him take off?"

"We'd better not." The words were kindly but spoken with unmistakable firmness. "We've lots to do, Melody."

"When do I start school?"

"Immediately. See that girl over there? The one with the furs?"

"She looks like a movie star."

"She is—a starlet. Watch her walk, and then try to walk exactly as she does. You stride, Melody, and it's most unfeminine."

"I'll—I'll try."

"There. That's better, much better." Mrs. Matthews held the door open for her and Melody walked into the warm California sunshine. Melody's panic ebbed. The world seemed a bright place, the sky blue. Even the palm trees were exciting. "Here's our car," Linda said.

A chauffeur opened the door of the long blue Cadillac for them. They drifted away, riding as though on air.

Golly Melody thought. She leaned forward, watching a twin-engine airplane take to the sky. Once again she felt her throat tighten with emotion.

Mrs. Matthews smilingly asked, "Have a nice flight down?"

"Yes. I like flying. Especially with Kenney." Melody did not tell Mrs. Matthews that Kenney was the only pilot she had ever flown with.

"He's such a nice boy." Linda Matthews settled back, looking critically at Melody. "We've so much to do. Not that you aren't beautiful as you are. But we must improve, improve, improve. We can always improve, Melody."

"I want to."

"Of course. It's fortunate for you that Mr. Ransome is taking such an interest in you."

"Yes ma'am, I know."

"Melody, don't bleat like that."

Melody's eyes opened wide at the sharp tone. "Don't what?"

"There you go again, bleating just like a sheep. Don't say 'Yes, ma'am' like that. If you must, say, 'Yes, Mrs. Matthews.'"

Oh, brother, Melody thought. "Yes, Mrs. Matthews," she said meekly.

Mrs. Matthews smiled happily. "That sounds so much better."

"Yes, Mrs. Matthews."

"How old are you, Melody?" The dark sharp eyes were going over Melody's lush curves and thrusting breasts.

"Nineteen, Mrs. Matthews."

"Oh, such a wonderful age." The dark woman placed her hand companionably on Melody's knee. "Such a wonderful age. I remember when I was nineteen with the world at my feet. The entire world." She sighed thoughtfully. "I'll try to keep you from making the same mistakes I made, Melody. Where did you go to school?" Her hand remained on Melody's knee and Melody could feel the warmth of the touch through her skirt.

"All over," Melody was purposely vague. She had never attended school regularly. For one thing, there had always been the clothing problem. She had hated going to school looking so different from the other kids. Also, even while Effie had been the breadwinner, they had moved around a lot. By the time Melody was earning money she was out of the habit of school.

"How far did you go in school?"

"I finished high school," Melody lied.

"What are your interests?"

"My interests?" Melody looked blankly at Linda Matthews.

"Your hobbies. What, do you do for fun, Melody?" Melody repressed a laugh. Fun? Maybe it was fun, sometimes, to outwit the wolves, to fight them off when they tried to possess her body. What else? She recalled the sleazy movie houses in a dozen scattered towns, and how they had smelled of body odors. She remembered chewing gum on the seats and candy wrappers on the floor and some fresh guy sitting next to her, rubbing his leg against hers every chance he got. But these were not things she could tell this beautifully dressed woman. "I haven't had much chance for fun," she said.

"You have a potentially good voice," Mrs. Matthews said thoughtfully, "and a lovely body. You could sing, Melody, and dance, too. Those long legs were made for dancing. All you need is the necessary training."

"I'm going to be a secretary," Melody said.

"Yes, of course. But there are secretaries—and secretaries. Mr. Ransome wants you to take voice and dancing as well."

"But won't I learn to type and take shorthand?"

"In due time."

The Cadillac rolled to a stop in front of a handsome apartment house. The chauffeur opened the door for them.

"Is this where I'm to live?" Melody asked breathlessly, looking up at the beautiful brick and glass building.

"While you're in my care," Mrs. Matthews said smilingly. She nodded to the driver. "That'll be all for today, Tony."

Tony touched his cap with deference but his black eyes were hungrily touching Melody. "Yes, ma'am," he said.

A doorman in a splendid wine-colored uniform opened the door for them. "Good afternoon, Mrs. Matthews," he said, as doormen had spoken greetings from the screens of those movie houses.

They walked into a softly lighted lobby. Melody's feet seemed to sink into the springy carpeting. A pert girl jumped to her feet from a reception desk and came smilingly to meet them.

"Jane, this is Melody Frane," Mrs. Matthews introduced them. "Melody, Jane Carwell. All the girls take turns on the desk."

Jane took Melody's hand. She said cordially, "So happy you're to join us, Melody." She turned to the older woman. "Anita's in now. She knows that Melody will be her roommate."

"Excellent. Melody and I will have a chat in my apartment, Jane. Please don't let us be disturbed."

"Right," Jane said. Again she smiled at Melody. "So happy to have met you."

"Thank you," Melody acknowledged. What lovely manners Jane had—Melody was determined that she would watch Jane Carwell and try to imitate her.

In Mrs. Matthews' apartment, a spacious and restful place, a maid served tea. Mrs. Matthews spoke slowly. "This is an apartment for career girls," she said. "For the most part, they're television and movie starlets. You'll get to know them all eventually, but right now I want you to be selective."

"Ma'am?" Melody felt awkward, trying to balance the teacup on one knee and munch a cookie at the same time.

"Don't bleat, Melody."

"Yes, Mrs. Matthews."

"I mean for you to keep to yourself—just at first, of course. Your roommate, Anita Ford, will help you a good deal. Listen to her and learn from her. She knows as much about you as I do."

"Yes, Mrs. Matthews."

Mrs. Matthews sipped her tea expertly. "Now Melody, we have certain ground rules here which must be observed. On the matter of dates—you can't date, period."

"Yes, Mrs. Matthews. I don't know any boys here."

Mrs. Matthews uttered a silvery little laugh. "That's no problem for a beautiful girl like you, Melody. Some will try—but you must remember this one important rule—no dates. Without my permission, that is. Perhaps later we'll arrange something for you."

"Yes, Mrs. Matthews."

"You must be in the building by ten p.m. No exceptions, Melody. Remember these simple rules and you won't have any trouble."

"I'll remember," Melody promised.

"Then, when you've finished with your tea, we'll go up and meet your roommate, Anita Ford."

Anita Ford, a dark-haired girl with olive skin, wore a green terrycloth robe and no shoes or stockings. She had a slender, boyish figure. When Mrs. Matthews had left them together, Anita arched her black brows at Melody.

"What do you think of Bloody Mary?" she asked.

"Who?"

"Bloody Mary is what we call Mrs. Matthews around

here. Not to her face, of course."

"She's very refined," Melody said. She was still tingling with the excitement of her initial exposure to Beverly Hills and Hollywood and the life Harry Ransome had mapped out for her.

Anita chuckled. "You could call her that," she admitted, "among other things. She's an old actress, though she wouldn't like my calling her old. She actually starred in movies before they had sound, before people spoke on the screen, if you can imagine. She was famous once."

"She's kinda—kinda fussy."

"You haven't seen anything yet. But she knows show business and she knows her way around Hollywood."

"Are you an actress?"

Anita's boyish, friendly chuckle sounded again. "Trying to be. I'm getting a few parts now in the Lonely Man series, thanks to Mrs. Matthews."

"Gee, I used to watch that—when I got a chance." A chance, she meant, to look at someone else's television set. Some migratory workers had TV sets—though not many of them.

"I'm going out tonight with a man who is assistant director on another show," Anita said, unbelting her robe and, without self-consciousness, draping it over a chair. As she walked nude around the room, Melody watched her wide-eyed. The olive skin had a satiny smoothness and the unbelievably small waist curved into a slender arch of hip. Anita's tummy was flat as a pancake. She moved about gracefully, selecting her clothing. She talked as she dressed.

"I came to California two years ago from a little town in Illinois. I thought I was ready for TV and movies. I wound up as a waitress in a drive-in until Mrs. Matthews saw me and agreed to take me on. I've been fairly busy since, but it's not an easy life, being one of her girls. She runs you every single moment. Like tonight. She had to pass on my date before I could accept. She won't let me see a man who can't help my career. That's one of her ground rules, as she calls them. Well, she's been successful. You'd be surprised at some of the stars who owe their stardom to Mrs. Matthews. Every now and then they come back and give us all a pep talk. It's exciting— sometimes. Boring most of the time. You sort of get used to it."

Anita stopped in front of the mirror and surveyed herself with critical eyes.

"Gee, you look lovely," Melody said breathlessly.

Anita turned, frowning thoughtfully. "This town is full of lovelies," she said. "You're a little special, though. I don't know what it is—but if I had your figure and your looks, I wouldn't have a worry in the world."

"But you're prettier than I am," Melody declared honestly.

Anita kept looking at Melody. "If you wanted, you could have a lot of boy friends."

"There's just one I really want," Melody said. "He's a pilot in Arizona."

"Pilots are fun. But they drink too much and usually

they're after just one thing."

"I know," Melody said.

"Well, I haven't given you the entire pitch. There are forty of these efficiency apartments in this building with two girls in each apartment. The pool is between the wings. We take turn on the reception desk downstairs. But you won't have to worry about that for at least a month."

"A month?" Melody exclaimed. "I thought I'd be back to work in Arizona in a month."

Anita looked puzzled. "Back to work? In Arizona? Aren't you one of Mrs. Matthews' girls?"

"I don't know," Melody said hesitantly. She actually did not know what to tell Anita. "I'm being sort of groomed for a special job," she added lamely.

"Well, what do you know? But no matter. We have two drama classes a week and two dance periods. And watch both those teachers, Melody, they're ravenous, especially toward a virginal dish like you." Anita had finished dressing and now she drew on her gloves. "Good night, Melody. It's been so nice meeting you. I know we'll enjoy each other."

After Anita left Melody felt lonely. She wondered what her mother was doing. She thought about Kenney as she prepared for bed. She wished she were with him, feeling his strong arms around her and his hard demanding body against hers. She snapped out the light and crawled into bed. Her tears wet her pillow before she drifted off to sleep.

SIX

Melody found she had no time for tears of self-pity or anything else. Mrs. Matthews kept her busy.

On Monday they went shopping for clothes for Melody in the fashionable shops on Wilshire Boulevard. Melody spent three hours in a beauty salon. When Tony, the chauffeur, drove them back to the Latonia Apartments, the car was loaded with clothes—pretty clothes, casual clothes, dress-up clothes, and filmy lace underthings that Melody had never dreamed of owning. So much was happening, and happening so swiftly, that the past was crowded out of Melody's mind.

On Tuesday she reported to her dramatics teacher. His name was Emile Frontenac. Melody took the bus out to his studio on Hollywood Boulevard. She climbed a flight of stairs and waited in an anteroom. From beyond an unadorned wall she could hear a low murmur of voices. After a while a young woman in slim-jims came from some inner room. Her pseudo-jeans, unlike Melody's old ones, made her look sophisticated, poised and beautiful.

"I'll see you Thursday, Emile," she said in a husky voice, glancing at Melody as she swept by. Behind her she left an aura of expensive perfume.

A neat, compact man with a small black mustache appeared in the office doorway. He smiled. "You're

Melody," he said. He sounded French and he sounded like the movies.

Emile took her hand and kissed it. His mustache tickled. He kept his mouth on her hand for a long time. Beneath his receding hairline, his forehead was spattered with big brown freckles. Such hair as he had was short and bristly and black as velvet.

He stood erect and looked into Melody's eyes. His own eyes were curiously gray and yellow and Melody had an impression that he was not healthy. But he was different—and the difference fascinated her. He kept her hand in his as he led her into his inner office, a simply furnished but somehow soothing place. He indicated that she was to relax on a couch so the light from the window was full on her face. He sat in the shadows and studied her.

"You are a beautiful girl, Melody," he said finally in his funny French accent. "Beautiful I say, not pretty." The words had a businesslike ring—this appraisal was part of his job.

"Thank you," Melody said.

He shook his head impatiently. "Please not to interrupt. I am the teacher. You must recognize me as the teacher, Melody. You must always do as I say. Always. You understand?"

"Yes," Melody said, although she was not sure she understood fully. She remembered Anita's warning and made a mental reservation that she would go only so far in this obedience thing.

"Good. Now we begin. You know what is Drama?"

His tone made a name of the last word.

Melody shook her head.

"That is good. I always like it so. Drama is re-creation of life. It is a form of literature and has the longest history of any of the arts. More than five thousand years ago, the Egyptians celebrated the coronation of their kings by dramatic re-enactment."

Melody yawned.

Emile Frontenac stared sternly at her. "What I say is boring?"

Melody protested, "No, sir. I've had such a busy week."

Frontenac sprang to his feet and paced like a restless cat. "Always, such a busy week. Then they come to Emile's studio to rest. This is too much. Even for a rich man such as your Ransome." He wheeled, and came to the couch to sit beside her. He took her hand in both of his. "We must work together, Melody. You understand. We must establish rapport?" He leaned closer. She felt his breath on her cheek. His knees pressed against her legs.

"Yes, sir," she said meekly. But the look in his eye reminded her of the field hands. She would have to watch him.

He dropped her hand abruptly and stood up. "Western drama," he said, "comes, you understand, from ancient Greece. Was the grape harvest good? Then they must celebrate the feast of Dionysus. The people danced and sang through the streets of the country groves. They made wild bacchanalian processions." With vigor, grace and no self-consciousness, Frontenac demonstrated what he meant. He stopped his gyrating and continued. "But when the harvest is not so good, only those who can make believe will want to celebrate. And so we have wandering troupes, going from city to city, to retell the story of Dionysus in dance, in songs, in pantomime. They were the true ancestors of modern actors and actresses." He paused, frowning heavily, and repeated with distasteful intonation, "Modern actors and actresses. Cheese. Wood."

He took a bulky notebook from his bookcase and put it in Melody's hands. "This is a copy of Bourdet's The Prisoner. It is an artful study of a lesbian."

"What is a lesbian?" Melody asked.

Emile stared. "What is a lesbian, you ask? You do not know what is a lesbian?"

"No. Should I?"

"So we have the babe in the woods, eh, no?" Suddenly his eyes seemed more yellow than gray. "We must educate you, Melody, my lovely young pupil."

Melody was not sure she wanted to be educated. She kept remembering what Anita had said about Emile and the dancing teacher. She wanted to pull her hand away from Emile's grasp but she was afraid of offending him.

He amplified, "Lesbianism means homosexual relations between women."

"Oh, you mean a queer? Why'nt you say so?"

"The term," Emile continued more coldly, "comes

from the behavior of the ancient inhabitants of the Island of Lesbos."

"What did they do?" Melody asked.

"What did they do? They did everything, Melody. The women reversed at their pleasure the roles of men and women. In modern times, this condition may be a woman's attempt to avoid feelings of inferiority or anxiety when she compares herself with a male."

"A woman just can't be a man," Melody declared.

"Melody, you are quaint." He sat closer, placed his arm around her waist. "But back to the drama. As you perhaps have guessed, I like the French dramatists. Now read from Bourdet, on the pages I have marked. Read with great expression, for now you are the heroine of this play. You are not Melody Frane. When you act, you make a world and your world is the only real one. Read."

Melody read three lines, her face flaming. Then she had to stop. She said, "Oh, I can't pretend I'm like that. Anyway, it's not a very good mimeographing job."

Emile took the manuscript and put it aside. "No, it is not a very good reproduction," he said gently. "We have started too abruptly, Melody. We must get to know each other, then we will start again." He slipped to the floor at her feet and took off her highheeled pumps. He pulled her leg out full length, took her foot in his hand and kissed it. He kissed her feet and ankles. He kissed her calves and knees. She felt a drowsy euphoria overcoming her as his kisses reached higher. She suddenly thought of Kenney and pushed

Emile away.

He rose, still poised and unruffled. "Perhaps we proceed at too fast a pace." He took another volume from his bookcase, this time a thin one, bound in leather. "We start with poetry, Melody. Read this. Study it. Be a participant as you read. This is dramatic poetry. You will read it aloud to me when we meet again." He knelt and slipped on her shoe and ardently kissed her ankle again. "You must be ready," he said.

Melody left the studio, feeling far from ready. She walked along Hollywood Boulevard in the dazzling sunshine, wondering if Emile was crazy, but with excitement still fluttering through her. What a strange little man. Lesbianism. She shuddered, not wanting to think of the things Emile had put in her head, yet unable to help herself.

She walked the sunny street, trying to work off her excitement. When she reached the window of an art shop, she stopped and looked at the paintings. In this city, everyone but Melody Frane seemed to be creative. She could not even type.

The doorway adjacent to the art supply store, she noticed, belonged to a business college. Impulsively, she entered. A prim girl in glasses smiled at her mechanically from the reception desk.

"I want to see about taking a business course," Melody said.

"Please be seated. Our Mr. Dana will see you shortly."

Mr. Dana proved to be a tall, tweedy man who wore heavy glasses. He looked very confident behind a huge gleaming desk in his small, plain office.

"I only have Mondays off," Melody explained. "I thought I could take shorthand and typing and perhaps some office procedure." She had read the school brochure while waiting to see Mr. Dana.

He showed very white teeth in a very brown face. The expression, she realized, was meant to be a smile. "That's quite an order for one day a week."

"I'm a fast learner," Melody said. She had learned to sort melons in just one day, a skill most girls took a week or more to acquire.

"I'm sure you are," Mr. Dana said. "But this is a course that demands daily—or nightly—attendance."

"I could attend in the evening," Melody said. "But I have to be home by ten o'clock every night."

Mr. Dana thought that could be arranged, he said. When Melody left she had signed up for an accelerated business course. If Mr. Ransome had not made plans to cover her secretarial training, she would do it herself, she thought. She certainly had to be prepared to take over as Mr. Ransome's secretary when the time came.

Harry Ransome, she had learned that morning, had already put her on salary and quite a nice salary at that. Mrs. Matthews had given her her first check before they went out shopping.

Everything that was happening to her, Melody thought, was fantastic, hard to believe. She was a lucky girl.

She still felt lucky when she fell asleep that night,

with Anita sitting beside her on the bed, chatting a mile a minute.

Trying to listen to her roommate, Melody lapsed into a kind of wide-eyed dream, almost an illusion. She moved through Los Angeles in the dream, surrounded by marvelous little miracles. A white convertible with its top down passed on the glittering dream street and she wished she were driving the car. Instantly she was seated behind the steering wheel. She seemed to be wearing skinny gold lame jeans.

She grew tired of the white convertible and the shining pants. She saw a beautiful girl walking with a tall man. She wished, without envy, that she were the girl. She became the girl. She looked up lovingly at the man. He was Kenney.

Suddenly the Kenney in her dream spoke with a French accent. "I am Emile Frontenac," Kenney said. "This is Drama, the oldest of all the arts."

Crossly, she willed him to be Kenney, the real Kenney. But the dream faded.

SEVEN

Melody's dancing teacher was named Bart Cameron. He was a big-shouldered, tough-looking man with unruly brown hair. He reminded her of Kenney in a way, but more of Burt Lancaster, the movie actor. In this town, she was beginning to find, everyone looked like some actor or actress. Cameron had the Lancaster intensity of expression. His rugged face was pitted with tiny pock marks. He looked critically at Melody at their first meeting and said, "You're built to dance, girl. How tall—never mind, I'll take your measurements."

"Now?" Melody asked nervously.

"Not this very minute," he said, grinning at her. "Put on your leotards first. Dressing room just through that door and to your right. Hurry."

Melody got into leotards. She felt naked, although the cloth covered her from head to foot. The leotards fitted too tightly, she thought, although Mrs. Matthews had selected them and had approved of the way they looked. She returned to the studio, where Mr. Cameron was waiting.

He asked her to turn around several times. She followed instructions self-consciously.

"Relax," he commanded irritably. "I'm not going to bite you."

"I can't relax," she said in a small voice. "I feel too— too exposed."

He laughed, "You'll get over that."

"I hope so."

"Of course you will. Stand over by the bars."

She obediently stood by the exercise bars. He began taking her measurements with a tape. He measured her neck, arms, bust, waist, and the length of her legs.

She disliked the process, which made her feel that her body was not quite hers any more.

"Be still," he commanded, jabbing his left hand into her crotch and stretching the tape to her ankles. He rose and said intensely, "You're a remarkably well-built young woman, Melody. Did you ever dance?"

"No. Not at all."

"Well, you're old to start dancing, but we'll see. If I'd got you ten years ago—" His voice broke off. When he spoke again, he gave her rapid-fire instructions about limbering up on the bar. Then he left her to exercise.

She worked conscientiously, and soon found that she was sweating. The feeling was a good one. Her body was used to effort. She had not really perspired since leaving Arizona.

She remembered the touch of Cameron's hands as he measured her body. For some reason she found the memory more pleasing than the fact. What in the world would Kenney think of her? She dismissed him from her mind and went on with the exercises. She found some muscles she had not known she owned.

Bart Cameron interrupted her half an hour later. He led her into a small sterile-looking chamber off the exercise room and pointed to a padded table.

"Your muscles will be sore," he warned. "I'd better give you a rubdown. That will alleviate some of the soreness."

He took a sheet from a cabinet and handed it to her.

"Take off your leotards and get on the table under the sheet," he said. "I'll be back in five minutes." He left the room.

She got on the table, stripped the leotards off and

pulled up the sheet.

When Cameron returned he was naked to the waist. He said shortly, "Roll over on your tummy."

She rolled over. He moved the sheet upward and began massaging her legs with a pleasant-smelling oil. "We must watch your legs," he said. "Mustn't let them get bulgy with muscles. These legs are too beautiful to neglect." His hands were firm, yet velvety. The strong fingers, kneading, rubbing, brought her a warm glow and yet she felt disturbed.

"Maybe you'd better quit," she suggested.

He stopped massaging her and pulled the sheet down. "You don't like it?"

"Yes. Maybe too much."

He chuckled and patted her shoulder. "You're too honest to be a girl," he said, "but you really are all girl, very much all girl. I like you, Melody, and I think we'll get along fine. Just remember to do everything I tell you."

"I will."

"All right for now. There's a shower in the next room. Shower and rub yourself briskly with the towel. I'll see you next Wednesday. In the meantime, stick with the exercises I showed you. Every day, morning and night."

"I will," Melody promised.

A tall man waited on the street outside the dance studio. He moved toward her as she left the building.

She cried "Kenney," and ran to him.

He swept her up in his arms and kissed her on the

mouth. Several pedestrians paused.

"Kenney," she whispered in confusion, "not here on the street."

"They'll think we're making a movie," he declared. "See 'em looking around for a camera?" His eyes were hungry. "I've been dreaming of this. Let's step in this drugstore, get a cold drink and do a little gabbing." He paused to admire her. "You look terrific, Melody."

She blushed. "I always hated men to look at me like that. But from you I like it."

He guided her into the drugstore. "You're prettier than ever," he said fervently, "if that's possible."

They found a booth and seated themselves. Kenney took both her hands in his and held them tightly. "I've sure missed you, Melody, honey."

"I've missed you, too," she admitted.

"Enough?" he asked meaningly.

"I'm not sure," she said in a troubled voice.

"Happy down here?"

"It's very exciting," she said. "It's dreams coming true. I guess I love it, Kenney, every single minute."

He frowned. "I guess you do," he said.

"What are you doing in California?"

"I brought the boss down. You'll probably see him tonight." His frown deepened. "At least, that's what I gathered from the little he said."

"Don't look so gloomy. I can handle him, Kenney."

"Can you?"

"Sure I can. Have you seen—seen Ma lately?"

Kenney hesitated before saying bluntly, his face

sober, "She stays drunk all the time."

"Kenney, where does she get the money?"

He did not reply.

Melody continued, "She isn't—alone?"

"You kidding? Somebody ought to kill that snake, Joe Priddy."

"Gosh, life was so good," Melody said, feeling close to tears. "All I have to do is think about Ma and all the fun is gone."

He squeezed her hand across the table. "Honey, don't punish yourself. Your Ma has got her own life to live and you've got yours."

"She's my mother."

"Don't I wish she wasn't," Kenney said heatedly. "But she's your mother all right and if you'd let her, she'd be mine too. Maybe if I was her son-in-law I could bring her out of it."

"She's sick, Kenney. I don't think you or anyone else can help her, except a doctor. Maybe some day—"

"I'd like to try, anyway," Kenny said doggedly. "Being married to me wouldn't be so bad, Melody. I just bought a duster out of my wages. Dusting crops is a good business. I could go into business for myself."

She felt her dreams threatened—even her dreams about Kenney.

"Oh, Kenney," she said breathlessly. "That's the most dangerous kind of flying. You told me so yourself."

"Not when you're careful and wear a crash helmet. And I always wear one. How about it Melody?"

"I don't want to hurt you," she said in a low voice.

She had been hurt and disappointed so many times herself that she could not bear to see someone else injured.

"You're going ahead with this deal with Ransome?" he asked grimly.

"For now. How did you find me, anyway?"

"A thin, dark-haired girl at the Latonia told me where you would be. Her name's Anita."

"My roommate. Isn't she nice?"

"Too skinny for me." Kenney grinned again. "I like 'em more along your lines, honey."

"How long can you stay in L.A.?"

"Just until the morning, I guess. The boss made a quick trip down for some reason, I don't know exactly what. He doesn't confide in me."

A wave of homesickness engulfed her. "Oh, I want to see you," she said, "to be with you for just a little while. Alone."

"Maybe we can manage." Kenney sounded suddenly unsteady. He slid a card across the table to her. "This is where I'm staying, a motel near the airport. Soon as the boss lets you go, get a cab and come over."

The waitress brought their cokes. They toasted one another silently, as though making a pact.

EIGHT

Melody's first reaction, when she saw Harry Ransome again, was surprise. In a conservative business suit Ransome was not as impressive as when he wore scuffed cowboy boots and stiffly starched khaki. He looked like a middle-aged businessman instead of a land baron.

He and Melody met in his hotel suite. He surveyed her appraisingly. "You're developing," he said in a pleased voice. "More than I had hoped for, Melody."

"I'm glad," she said. "And I really do appreciate the opportunity you're giving me, Mr. Ransome—"

"Harry, remember?" he reminded her. He took her hands in his and kissed her mouth. His lips felt cold. She shuddered. He seemed much older than he had been in Arizona. She noted for the first time that the flesh hung from the underside of his jaw.

"Yes, Harry."

He had ordered champagne in a bucket. With a flourish he popped a cork, explaining, "Talk and wine belong together—and we have something to talk about. I need your help, Melody, on a little business deal."

"Oh, yes, Harry. Anything you say." She looked forward to telling him about her business course.

He poured champagne into fragile, long-stemmed glasses, touched his glass to hers and nervously gulped down the sparkling liquid. Melody tasted her drink and was not sure she liked its slightly sour quality. Champagne, she thought, was a beautiful word to say and a beautiful drink to look at. All she had against champagne was the taste.

Harry poured himself another drink, sat on the edge of a blue divan and motioned her to sit beside him.

"This job," he said, "will come up in a couple of weeks. We'll see if Mrs. Matthews can give you some time off." He paused. Melody was wearing what Linda Matthews had called a late day dress, a sheath of black raw silk, high-necked in front, sleeveless and practically backless, and sashed with a thin belt of gold leather. "You have style," he said. "Will you use it for me? Style can be important."

"Whatever you say, Harry," Melody said quietly, more than a little puzzled.

Suddenly he took the glass from her hand. He put the glass on the coffee table. "I'm tired," he said. "We'll talk business later." His arms started to close about her—then he released her abruptly. "Let's get comfortable, baby."

She watched him take off his coat. "I'm already comfortable," she said warily.

"For Pete's sake," he said crossly. He pushed her down on the divan with an impatience that matched the old-man droop of his jowls. He lay beside her and started to caress her. His body was strong and brown, a stark contrast to her ivory beauty. He pulled her dress away.

"Listen," she tried to protest. "Harry, please listen—" but his mouth stopped the words. She had once more that helpless sense he gave her of subjugation, of being mastered. He took her as though by right, and she endured his triumphant conquest of her body with shame for the pleasure she felt.

Her eyes closed and after a long while she opened them. Harry was beside her, breathing deeply and quietly. She felt sick and degraded. Was he asleep?

She got up carefully and put on her dress and coat. She left the suite.

She still had a date with Kenney tonight. What would he think of her, if he knew what she had done? What was becoming of her? Was she turning into a bum? Once she had wanted a place to run to—what she needed now was a place to have come from, the land of place nice girls came from, girls whose parents love them ...

"The International Motel," she told her taxi driver. She sank back against the seat. She must tell Kenney the score, give him a chance to break off with her—

Kenney took her coat and kissed her lips. "I didn't know if you'd make it any more," he said with obvious relief. "It's pretty late."

Tell him the truth, prompted her inner voice.

"I wanted to come sooner," she said, "but I couldn't."

"What'd Ransome want with you?"

Tell him. Be fair with him.

She laughed. "He never did tell me exactly. A job in

about two weeks. I'll know more later, I guess. He just wanted to make sure I didn't make other appointments—like my lessons."

"Would you like a drink?"

"No, nothing. You have a beer if you like."

Kenney found himself a can of beer, took a sip and put the can down.

"I don't really want a beer," he said.

She put out her arms and he came to her and they kissed. She liked his kisses—and besides, they prevented conversation. She could tell him some other time—about herself and Harry Ransome. Meanwhile, she was making him happy. His lips touched her ear and his hands explored her body.

She felt warm and loved. An onrush of desire coursed through her veins and nerves. "Let me undress," she whispered fiercely. She reached for the zipper of her black silk gown.

"Want me to turn out the light?" he asked.

"No," she breathed. "I want you to see me. All of me."

His coppery eyes had a dimly thunderous look as she lifted the gown over her head and pulled it off. She knew her skin was creamy smooth, flawless as polished ivory. She delighted in showing him the beauty of her breasts.

The longing in his eyes heightened her desire. She stepped daintily out of her panties, unfastened her bra and let it drop. She stood against him. His hand slid down her back and rested on the smooth round of her buttock.

His lips touched her skin. She pressed his head against her. He muttered a strangled sound and picked her up in his hard arms and carried her to the bed. She opened her arms to receive him.

For a while he was part of her and she was part of him. She could not bear the thought of releasing him. Nothing mattered beyond the lock of their union. She heard their breathing, the thunder of their hearts.

After a long time, their breathing lessened and they lay side by side in the brief contentment of consummated love.

"Kenney?" she asked finally.

"Yeah?" His arm was about her. His eyes were half closed.

"You're not sleepy?"

"No, honey."

"How do you feel?"

"Relaxed as an old dishrag" he said peacefully.

"Was it good?"

"The best, and you know it."

"Better than anyone you've ever had?" she continued anxiously.

"Much the best."

"Have there been many others?"

"None that mattered. The difference is how I feel about you, Melody."

"How do you feel about me?"

He rolled to his side and looked at her out of wide coppery eyes. "I love you," he said. "I've never said that to another girl in my life. With you, everything is different. I want to protect you, I want you to be as close to me as my heart. Sometimes I feel I want to button you up inside me and keep you."

His words buried her memories of Harry Ransome's lust. She bit gently at his ear. "I'm glad," she said.

"But it doesn't make any difference? You're still going to play this little game with Harry Ransome?"

They must not speak of Ransome—not now. Her arms went around his neck and she pulled his head down between her ivory breasts with their dark tips. "Don't be angry with me, darling."

"What do you want me to do?"

"Just love me," she said simply.

"Now, right now, again?"

"Yes, right now. Can you, honey?"

"I think so."

Clean me, part of her thought. Let your love he fire and flood, to burn away his kisses and wash away my shame ...

She held him tighter, writhing against him, trying to goad his passion.

"Oh, you can," she whispered. "You can, darling, you must—" Her hands slid down his back, clutching him to her. She had roused him. With a harsh sigh of pleasure, he took her once more.

From now on, she thought fervidly, life would pay her back for all the lost, sad hours. She needed Harry Ransome, she recognized dimly, for the luxuries that were quickly becoming a habit—for lovely clothes, for taxi fare, for pure carefreedom.

And she needed Kenney for love.

She needed both men.

Don't think, she warned herself. Just enjoy the moment—in Kenney, in his strength ...

NINE

At five A.M., Melody left the taxi and darted across the sidewalk into the Latonia Apartments. The doorman was off duty and no one was on the desk in the lobby of the building. She took the self-service elevator to the third floor and silently let herself into her apartment.

She undressed in the haggard light of dawn and scurried into bed. Suddenly Anita sat up in the other twin bed and switched on the bed lamp.

"Home at last," she pronounced with a yawn. She looked curiously alert. "Bloody Mary was upset, to say the least."

"She knew I didn't come in?" Melody asked weakly.

Anita lit a cigarette with a gold lighter. "She knows. And so does your sponsor—what's his name?— Ransome."

"Oh dear," Melody wailed. "I guess I have it coming."

"Where were you, anyway?"

"Out," Melody said slowly. "What can I tell Mrs. Matthews?"

"Not what you just told me," Anita advised. "She'll guess the worst if you don't make up a good alibi.

Don't be too honest, Melody. You'll get nowhere telling the truth."

"Great," Melody said unhappily. "I'm too dumb to lie to someone like Mrs. Matthews."

"You dumb? Nonsense. Now I've heard everything."

"No, I mean it. I'm not smart at all, not like you and Jane and the rest of the girls here."

"You have something we'd all like to have. Freshness, Melody. You still enjoy being alive—and I'm not sure I do any more."

The telephone rang, a startling sound in the hush of early day.

Anita looked at Melody with arched eyebrows and lifted the pink telephone from its cradle. "Yes," she said, making a face. "Yes, Mrs. Matthews, she is. Yes, Mrs. Matthews, I'll tell her. You didn't disturb me at all, Mrs. Matthews."

She hung up the phone and frowned. "Bloody Mary wants to see you," she said. "In her apartment. Right away. Sounds ominous, Melody. But remember what I told you. Make up a good story and stick with it."

"I'll try," Melody promised. She began dressing again.

Both Linda Matthews and Harry Ransome were waiting when Melody arrived. The rancher smiled, but Linda Matthews did not.

She said, "When you arrived here, Melody, I told you —"

"Please, Mrs. Matthews," Ransome interrupted, holding up his hand. "This isn't necessary at all. I'm sure that Melody won't let it happen again."

"No, I won't," Melody said.

Ransome suggested, "What we all need is a cup of coffee."

After their hostess had gone into her kitchenette, Harry Ransome's smile vanished. He turned angrily to Melody. "Where the hell were you?" he asked.

"Out," she said. There was nothing else she could tell him.

For a moment, she thought he would hit her—and then a sour version of his smile returned. "I'll let it go at that," he allowed. "Maybe it's just as well for you to be a night bird—all things considered. I thought I'd better see you, even though it's early, before I leave for Tucson. I have an eleven o'clock appointment there today."

"Yes, sir, Mr. Ransome."

The cold blue eyes warmed fractionally with amusement. "It's still Harry, you know," he said in a soft and mocking voice.

"Yes, Harry."

"There's a man I want. I've tried to get him to leave his present employer and he won't do it. I think you can convince him that he ought to make a change."

"Me? Talk a man into changing jobs?"

"Yes, Melody, you. I've set things up for you. Two weeks from today, Kenney will fly you to Las Vegas. A limousine will meet you at the airport and take you to a certain motel where a room will be reserved for you. You'll walk in and make yourself at home. The man will join you there. His name is Frank Olney.

He's an engineer. I need him badly."

"He must be an important man."

"He is. He's invented a little electronic gadget that makes a missile lots more sophisticated. I want that little gadget—I want to get in the missile business. I'm depending on you, Melody."

Melody had an uneasy feeling that Harry Ransome was crazy. She said nothing.

"Just be there to meet him. I'll take care of the rest," Harry said reassuringly.

"Is that all?" she asked doubtfully.

"You'll do it for me?"

"I'm working for you, Harry. Whatever you want."

Mrs. Matthews returned with coffee. She seemed in a better mood. Before Harry Ransome left, he talked with her briefly at the door.

When they were alone, Mrs. Matthews came back to Melody and sat beside her. "I'm very surprised at your action, Melody, in breaking our rules. I'm disappointed. I thought you were lovely and sweet."

Melody flushed, not knowing what to say.

"If Mr. Ransome had not interceded," she continued, "I would have had to discipline you. However, we'll forget it this time. How do you like your regimen so far?"

"My what?"

"I've told you, Melody, don't bleat. If you don't understand something, merely say, 'I don't understand.'"

"Yes, Mrs. Matthews. And I don't understand."

"Your life, Melody. Your routine, the dance and drama lessons, your life here at Latonia with us."

"It's all wonderful," Melody said. "I can't believe it's happening to me."

Mrs. Matthews seemed satisfied. "Fine. You may go now, Melody. I'll arrange your schedule so you make take a few days in Las Vegas for Mr. Ransome."

"Thank you, Mrs. Matthews." Melody hesitated. "Do you know anything about this job he wants me to do?"

"That's entirely your business, my dear. And Mr. Ransome's." The older woman picked up cups and saucers. Melody was dismissed.

TEN

Ralph Dana, head of the Coast Secretarial School, was the only one of Melody's teachers who was disturbed by her request. Of course, he was the only one whom she herself had selected. He took off his horn-rimmed glasses and tapped them vexedly on his desk.

"You've just started with us, Melody," he said. "And according to your teachers, you're doing so well. Especially in shorthand."

"But I'll miss only a few classes," Melody protested. "I'll work hard to make them up. Maybe I can even make them up before I go."

He looked at her dossier, appearing not to have heard her. "Yes, especially shorthand. Do you play piano,

Melody?"

"No, sir."

"According to your teacher, your progress in shorthand is phenomenal. I just wondered—people with trained hands sometimes go ahead like that."

"I can play the guitar," Melody said. "I haven't played lately, but I know how."

Uncle Lance had taught her how to play a guitar.

He had been one of Effie's lovers, one of the better ones, a slim, lithe man with a weak face and a gentle drawl. He had taught Melody to play the guitar and had been kind to her, not pawing at her like a lot of them did. She had liked his quiet manners even when he was drunk—which was most of the time—and the way he drawled her name.

Lance had come into her life and gone out again, like the signposts along the highway as she moved north with the crops. With the eyes of memory, she could see his face so plainly, hear his voice and the chords of his guitar. How long had they been with him—a month, a year? She could not be sure any more. But the time had been her childhood, the only real childhood she had ever known.

"Let's step out and have a cup of coffee," Mr. Dana said, "and talk about this further. I'm interested in your problems."

"Why, thanks," Melody acknowledged.

She picked up her handbag and walked with him into the bright sunshine. They strolled down the street to the corner drugstore where, Melody had learned, some of the best problems in Hollywood were tackled over coffee.

They took a booth and Dana ordered. The booth was small and their knees touched under the table. Even Ralph Dana's knees, Melody mused, gave her an impression of his breeding and good education.

Tweedy knees.

"Melody," he asked, "what are you smiling about?"

She did not want to offend Ralph Dana. Suddenly shy, all she could say was, "I was thinking how kind you are to take an interest in me."

A surprising thing happened. His long face showed a flush of color, almost as though he were blushing.

"Listen, Melody. There's something you ought to know about yourself. This town is full of pretty girls —the prettiest in the world. A man stops noticing them after a few years. Suppose you lived near a plant nursery where you saw gorgeous flowers every day, year round—you'd never pay attention to one special rose. But if a wild flower came up some day, something different, something rare—you would notice."

She laughed. "You mean I'm like a wild flower? Where I lived before I came here, we had wild flowers, all right. But we called them weeds. And the cultivators cut them down and chopped them up between the rows of produce. You know what I've been most of my life, Mr. Dana? I've been a field hand. Since I was eleven, twelve, and big enough to lie about my age. That's another thing—I guess I'm not very truthful. And lately, I've been telling so many lies, to so many people, I'm beginning to be scared about it. Some day I'll wake up and I won't remember how much is a lie and how much isn't."

"Melody," he said earnestly, "do you know you're crying?"

"I thought I was laughing," she said. Suddenly she was telling him, because she had to tell someone, about the lies she was living with—the lies she was telling Kenney, or wanted Kenney to believe.

"I told him I was a virgin the first time he made love to me," she heard herself say. "Well, it was almost true—except that no girl is almost a virgin, I guess. And now he thinks he's the only man with me—and that's almost true, too. But Harry—he's sort of my sponsor—seems to feel he can have me any time he's in town. What am I turning into, Mr. Dana?"

Their knees still touched under the table. Although there was no physical resemblance, for an instant the business teacher's face reminded Melody of another face, remembered out of childhood—the face of Uncle Lance, the only one of Effie Frane's lovers who had given her real kindness.

The only man who had given her an inkling of what it might be to have a real father.

Ralph Dana sighed. "What are you turning into? I could tell you—except it would break my heart."

"Tell me," she begged. "Otherwise, I'll be scared."

He stopped looking like Uncle Lance. He looked like himself and he looked like all the other men she had met who would study her full soft shoulders and the full firm breasts below them. He wants me she thought simply. And he's ashamed of wanting me. But he won't stay ashamed.

"In this town," he told her, "if you're proud, if you're shrewd, if you don't set too low a price on yourself, I think you're likely to become a successful courtesan. You're beautiful, Melody—and you've got a native intelligence, a spark, that makes you different from girls who aren't quite as beautiful. You'll learn your way around. You'll get to have your own code of morals. You'll meet more rich men—fabulously rich men— and you won't have to lie any more, because your past will stop being a secret. You'll stop being ashamed. Your name will be a household word, a synonym for glamor and sex and fun—you'll even have husbands. Maybe three or four of them, all millionaires.

"You'll never grow old—because in a way you've never been young. But maybe that's the price we have to pay for success. I wouldn't know. I've never been successful—running a business school isn't a big deal."

"What about Kenney?" she asked anxiously. "Will he be one of my husbands?"

Ralph Dana said sadly. "Of course not. Six months from now, you'll barely remember his name."

"That's not true," she cried. "I guess I'd rather die than lose Kenney, Mr. Dana—"

"You've just told another lie, Melody. Though you may not know it's a lie. You won't want to die when you lose him, because you'll be someone else. You'll be sophisticated, you'll be worlds beyond him. You'll have something inside yourself—well, it may not be happiness—but who is happy?"

The drugstore seemed to blur. Melody found she no longer wanted coffee. "I feel bad," she said. "I feel awful. Maybe it's better not to know the truth. Except that I don't believe you. I—I—"

"Let's get out of here," the business-school teacher said in sudden alarm. "I didn't mean—Melody, you look as though you were going to faint."

"It will pass," she said, but he took her arm and led her out of the store and she had to cling to him to keep from falling. She wanted to lie down. Her head felt light. She had not known that emotion could have so strong an effect.

She was aware of their returning to the business school. Of lying down on the couch in Ralph's private office. Of his hands, stroking first her forehead, and then her cheek, and then her knees and thighs—

The faintness passed. She tried to sit up.

"You poor little kid," he said, still touching her, caressing her. He kissed her cheek, pushing her back on the couch. He kissed her lips. "Poor little gorgeous kid."

She protested weakly, "This isn't safe. We shouldn't stay here." But she found she wanted his sympathy and understanding, wanted them almost unbearably. Also, he was far from being an unattractive man, and his caresses were having a heady effect on her, sending little tremors of desire through her body. In another moment, she would rise and leave, she thought. First, she wanted to explain that she liked him and was grateful to him for liking her in return. After she had explained she would leave promptly—

"I'm not happy, either, Melody," he was saying. "Everything in my life is sort of second best. I wanted to be an actor—that's why I came to the Coast. But I wasn't good enough—so I'm running a business school, just as I did in Bridgeport, Connecticut. I wanted a woman to love and I had her for a while—I married her. And marriages don't last in this crazy, beautiful town. Melody, please be kind—"

If it was kindness to let him embrace her while his breath quickened and his body closed on hers, she was kind—

Gently he pushed her blouse aside, gently pulled down her skirt. He still was as gentle as her Uncle Lance had been while teaching her to play the guitar. But Lance had never manifested sexual interest in Melody—he had been the only person who ever had treated her like a child, who had given her the friendliness that adults give to children. Not even Melody's mother had treated her like a child.

Mouth to mouth, thigh to thigh, she found a hectic release with Ralph Dana, a pleasure that had little to do with love. This was not like the ecstasy she had known with Kenney—and totally unlike the half-mesmerized submission she gave to Harry Ransome. This passion she shared with Dana was as satisfying in its way as food she had eaten in hunger, or sleep she had snatched in exhaustion.

But she was losing something else and she knew what she was losing. Childhood. All she had had of childhood was a few months, perhaps a year—and now her childhood was taken from her by this man whose kindness reminded her of Effie's long-ago lover.

The tempo of his lovemaking changed as their bodies meshed. He turned savage, demanding, a male animal stronger and larger than she had known a man could be. She cried out in pain as his teeth sank into her shoulder and his hand cut off the cry as he cuffed her, not hurtfully, but with unmistakable domination.

A red mist seemed to envelop them. She dared not open her eyes.

She realized in amazement that his passion was unendurably protracted, until she thought she must die of the ecstasy and pain—she was an instrument that he played on as Lance had played on the guitar. Her nerves would snap out of sheer mad pleasure soon—like guitar strings—unless there was an ending ... Oh!

It was over.

She slowly came back to herself.

They righted their clothing. The office seemed strangely businesslike once more, as though what just had happened had been a dream.

Ralph Dana looked at her pleadingly, the animal force in him now all spent and gone. "I—I'm not sorry," he said. "You were wonderful. If I can ever show you a kindness in repayment—"

"You've shown me kindness enough," she answered

softly.

Baffled, frightened, hardly daring to ask herself what was becoming of her, Melody left the school.

Shorthand she thought. Typing. She had thought she would change herself, change her luck, by learning new skills. Maybe what you learned depended on who you were to begin with.

Maybe she would never be anyone but Effie Frane's lonely daughter.

She thought this new way of life of hers must shatter, now that she had faced a truth of sorts—

But the days followed one another, and the way of life endured.

And one morning, it was time for her to fly to Las Vegas to do a chore for Harry Ransome.

ELEVEN

"I'm uneasy," Melody said. She folded foamy nylon underwear into a light blue overnight bag. "Somehow, I just don't feel right. And I'm worried about what Kenney will say."

Anita lifted her dark head and gave Melody an amused look. "Don't be silly," she said. "I'd give almost anything to be in your shoes. Just think, a whole weekend in Las Vegas without Bloody Mary looking over your shoulder."

Melody did not tell Anita what she would be doing in Las Vegas. For one thing, Harry Ransome had given her a less than complete briefing. And she disliked thinking of the possibilities involved.

"It'll be nice all right," Melody said vaguely. "But I'll have to ride all the way there with Kenney. He's going to fly me up and back. And he'll ask questions."

"Has he asked you to marry him?" Anita wanted to know.

"A dozen times."

"You're too young to marry, Melody. I know you claim you're nineteen. You're not fooling me, though."

"My mother married when she was fifteen," Melody protested. "She was only sixteen when I was born." That was not quite true. Actually, Melody had been born just two months after Effie turned fifteen—and Effie had not been married. Melody knew that the real facts should not be told. She had kept her secret well.

"That's much too young," Anita said positively. "Why, I'm twenty-one and I don't feel ready for marriage. Not in the legal sense, at least." She giggled, moved closer to Melody. "I think I'll give you a goodbye kiss right now." She wrapped her arms around Melody and covered her mouth with a long kiss.

Melody tried instinctively to pull away. Then she found herself relaxing.

The kiss was not the kind two friendly girls might exchange. This was the kind of kiss a man might give a woman.

The kiss held for a long time. Anita's hand touched Melody's breast. Only then did Melody resist. She moved back, her eyes wide, her heart beating rapidly.

"Why did you do that?" she asked.

"Because I love you, because I wanted to," she heard Anita murmur.

Melody busied herself once more with her overnight case. She felt confused, uncertain. She heard Anita's breathing close behind her, felt the other girl's hand on her. She said quickly, "Not now, Anita, please not now. I—I don't want anything from you right now."

Anita's hand dropped. "I'm in no hurry," she said lazily. "You'll be back, Melody. We have lots of time."

There was a knock on the door and Melody hurried to answer, glad of the interruption. Tony, the chauffeur, stood there, cap in hand. He asked, "Ready to leave, miss?"

She was ready, Melody said. She waved to Anita and left the room. Tony carried her overnight case to the elevator. Melody was aware that her roommate stood in the hall looking after her until the elevator door slid shut between them.

At the airport she ran into Kenney's arms. He held her close to him for a long moment and then held her away and looked at her.

"You're looking real well," he said finally.

She could not say the same for Kenney. He looked leaner, harder. There were faint dark shadows under his eyes. She ignored the crowded waiting room and leaned against him, gathering strength from his strength. "You—you look tired," she said rubbing her cheek against his vivid green shirt.

He was briefly silent. Then he said, "We won't be able to take off for a while because of incoming traffic. Let's go have a drink."

He steered her through the crowd and into the airport coffee shop. He gave their order and leaned back, his coppery brown eyes tenderly soft with love.

She felt a sudden wistful surge of affection for him and put her hand on his hard brown fist. "What's the latest from Arizona?" she asked.

"Nothing but work. I told you I bought a duster. I made eleven hundred dollars the first week, in my spare time."

"Kenney, that's wonderful. I hope you don't overdo it. You really do look tired."

His face hardened. "If it's dough you want, I mean to get my share of it. Maybe that will make a difference."

"I—I wish I could explain."

"There's nothing to explain." His voice retained a certain brittle toughness. "You want nice things, lots of expensive—"

She cut him off swiftly. "How is Ma, have you seen her?"

She could tell he hated answering the question. "The way she's going, she won't last long, Melody. She's drinking herself to death. Between the bottle and Joe Priddy, she hasn't a chance."

"Oh, Kenney, where does she get it?"

"I can't be sure—but I think her liquor money comes

from Harry Ransome. And that guy does nothing—but nothing—out of the goodness of his heart Somehow or other I tie it in with the way he's bankrolling you into a plush job."

Melody felt a dull ache deep inside her. She knew why Ransome was keeping Priddy and her mother in liquor but she did not want to admit the truth to herself. She had failed, failed miserably. Simply cutting relations with her mother had solved nothing, either for Melody or Effie. She ached to tell Kenney the truth but she knew she could not. She wanted him to go on feeling about her as he did, wanted him to believe she was a girl he could marry. She needed the warmth of his love and yet—she was ambitious, too. He had been right about her hunger for expensive luxuries. The craving drove her on, making her do things she did not really want to do, making her the kind of person she did not really want to be. She sighed deeply. "When I left Ma," she said, "I thought I'd just wash her out of my hair and out of my mind. But I guess I can't do it. I still worry about her, and wonder what I can do."

"Maybe there's nothing you can do any more," he said with a cold, hard stare. "Listen—I'd still like to know why you're going up to Las Vegas. The boss just told me to pick you up and bring you back Sunday afternoon. There must be something cooking and I don't like the smell of it."

She patted his hand. "Business, darling. Mr. Ransome wants me to see an engineer he hopes will work for him."

"See an engineer? What does that mean? What do you know about engineering?"

She laughed uncertainly. "You make it sound so—so immoral. I'll just have dinner with the man, take in a show I suppose, and perhaps gamble a little—or watch him gamble. And every now and then I'll mention how nice it would be to work for Mr. Ransome."

"How cozy," he said sourly.

"Please don't take on like that, Kenney, honey. I don't like it much either, but I think I owe it to Mr. Ransome."

"You won't have any time for me," he said doggedly.

"Is that why you're being so cross with me?"

He did not reply. Instead, he looked at his watch. "I'd better check with flight control," he said, rising. "Wait for me here."

She watched him walk away with a certain possessive pride. He was so tall and handsome that people turned to look after him. She knew she loved him—yet she was terrified of the consequences if she married him. At the very least, Harry Ransome would find some means of punishing them, if she and Kenney got married.

He was back in five minutes. "It's all set," he said. "Let's go."

She sensed a subtle and puzzling change in him. They were silent as they walked to the plane. But as he helped her in, he said, "You'll have to sit with me up front. I'm hauling a load in the passenger compartment."

She slipped obediently into the co-pilot's seat, watched him expertly ease his big frame into the cramped space beside her. She glanced over her shoulder toward the rear of the plane. A canvas tarp covered some bulky thing that completely filled the passenger compartment.

Kenney started the engines and called for permission to taxi. The little speaker overhead droned out instructions. They began rolling. While they taxied, Kenney tested instruments. Melody thought he was strangely tense.

They reached take-off position on an allotted runway. Kenney spoke into his microphone. "Ready to go, tower," he said.

"Cleared for take-off," Melody heard from the loudspeaker. Kenney pushed both throttles forward. They roared down the runway and took to the air. He climbed swiftly toward distant mountains. The hazy background below grew hazier as they climbed.

"Here's your clearance, Kenney," the loudspeaker said. "Cleared to the Corpus Christi Control Area, to cruise at eleven thousand all the way."

Kenney snapped off the loudspeaker and put his earphones on. He acknowledged the clearance and turned his attention to the dials on his panel.

Melody grasped his arm. "Corpus Christi?" she said. "Kenney, the man said Corpus Christi. That's Texas."

He shook off her hand, not looking at her, and continued his adjustments.

"Kenney, answer me. Why are we going to Corpus

Christi?"

He flicked the switch that she recognized as the automatic pilot, slid the earphones off and leaned back in his seat. "You know what we're carrying back there, Melody?" He gestured with his thumb at the passenger compartment.

"How would I know?"

"Gas," he said. "Fuel, baby. We have enough to fly the Pacific if we feel like it. But we're not flying the Pacific, just the Gulf of Mexico. I'm taking you to the West Indies, baby. You and me, we're going to live in Cuba from here on out."

Cuba.

Kenney did not look wild-eyed nor out of control— but Melody knew that some kind of despair must have driven him half—or more than half—out of his mind.

Right now, she had to take care of them both. Emotionally if not mechanically, she was his automatic pilot.

TWELVE

In Melody's short life, at least so it seemed to her, she had moved from one crisis, one problem, to another crisis, another problem. Years of living with the migratory workers had sharpened her intuition in emotional trouble.

She knew she could not persuade Kenney to change his mind by using ordinary logic. His set and sullen face told her that logic was unwanted. She knew, too, that pleading would be futile at this point.

But one thing was sure—she did not want to go to Cuba. Her impressions of the sad little island had been gleaned from migratory workers who were refugees from the place—and she was sure that no American in his right and mind would think of Cuba as a haven.

"Gee," she humored Kenney. "What're we going to do in Cuba?"

He answered with quiet bitterness. "For years, I've worked for guys like Ransome. No-goods who wouldn't have a dime if they hadn't been born with money. But there's nothing they won't do if it adds to what they already have. Whatever they want, they take. I'm sick of it."

"You've thought about this before, Kenney?" she asked as calmly as she could. She had to keep calm, she reminded herself.

"Not before I knew you. Lately, yes. Ransome gave me hell last time we came down. He suspected you'd spent the night with me. He kept hinting at it, and he kept telling me how it was with you and him, the lying sonofabitch." He looked at her with desperation in his eyes. "He was lying, wasn't he, Melody?"

Ransome had not been lying. But this was no time to make Kenney hear a confession.

"I haven't had anything to do with him," she said, "except that I'm working for him, just like you."

"Well, anyway, he's made life hell for me. I thought

about quitting but that was no good. I knew that as long as I worked for him I'd be seeing you one way or another."

She felt a catch in her throat. She took his brown hand and pressed it to her lips. He jerked his hand away as though from too hot a surface.

"Don't do that," he said roughly. "It's all right for men to kiss women's hands but not the other way around."

At another time, she would have smiled at his boyishness. "I just felt like it," she said in a small voice. She studied him for a long moment. "Then flying to Cuba isn't something you've been wanting to do for a long time?"

"A long time? Baby, Kenney Ward doesn't want anything for a long time. He goes after what he wants —and gets it."

"But why Cuba?" she pressed. *Calm. Stay calm.*

"Well, take this plane. With all its equipment it's worth roughly a quarter of a million dollars. If I take it any other place in the world but Cuba, the authorities would return it. And me, too."

"Cuba isn't a very good place to live," she pointed out musingly. "There isn't enough food for the people who are already there. And anyone who gets out of line gets shot."

"Nobody is going to push me around," he scoffed. "Not here and not in Cuba."

"Then why leave this country," she asked, "if you won't be pushed around?"

"Oh, hell, Melody," he said tiredly. He spent the next few minutes retrimming the airplane, which was already perfectly trimmed. He slumped back in his seat and looked stonily out into space.

"Maybe the Cubans won't like you coming there," she said.

He said nothing.

"They'll take the plane," she said, "if they want it. They'll throw you in prison if it suits them. And what will they do with me?"

He looked at her with reluctant returning sense. With no conviction, he said, "I have a friend high in the Cuban Air Force. This guy used to fly with me. He'll see that I get a fair shake."

"Anyone in the Cuban Air Force has lost his citizenship if he's an American," she said. "Anybody like that isn't reliable, Kenney."

"Well, Buzz Dalton is reliable. He's an old Army buddy."

"Maybe he was reliable when you knew him. That was a long time ago, wasn't it, Kenney?"

He did not answer.

They flew in silence for thirty minutes. The Grand Canyon showed below them. He used the microphone to report their position and then lapsed into another period of silence.

"You say you love me," she said. "I don't believe it."

"Of course I love you or I wouldn't be doing this. I can't let you ruin your life, Melody."

"Then you must believe some of the things Harry

Ransome told you."

"I didn't say that."

"But you must believe him—or you wouldn't be carrying me off like this."

"No, I just want you all for myself. I don't stand a chance against Ransome's millions. This is the only way I can have you."

"Haven't you already had me?" she asked quietly.

"That's different. I want you, all of you, just for me."

"There's an easier way than this," she insisted.

He looked at her without resentment for the first time since they had taken off. "What do you mean by that?"

"You know I love you," she said, "or I wouldn't have given myself to you. You know I wouldn't do that for anyone else."

"And so?"

"I'm awfully young to get married. I'd have to get Ma's consent."

"Yeah?"

"Well, there's time for both of us to prepare for marriage. I can go on with my studies. You can go on making extra money with your dusting. When the time is right for both of us, we can get married. We'd never be happy in Cuba. We'd always want to come back."

She watched him in silence as the crazy plan lost its grip on his mind. She leaned toward him and put her arms around his neck. She kissed him and closed her eyes. He responded for a long moment and then he pushed her away.

"Nothing you can say or do will change my mind," he said childishly.

In Melody's life there had been little space for tears. She had found them a waste of time. Yet now she could not help herself. She put her face in her hands and cried.

Kenney tried to straighten her hunched shoulders. She shook off his hands. "Don't touch me," she choked. "You don't love me. You just want to own me."

She heard his sigh of resignation. He spoke into his microphone. "Phoenix Control, Phoenix Control. I want to change my flight plan, please, and divert to Las Vegas."

She turned her tear-wet face to him. He took her in his arms, stroking her hair and whispering, "Don't cry, Melody, baby. Don't ever cry."

Melody barely had time to say goodbye to Kenney at the airport before the black limousine whisked her toward the roaring town of Las Vegas. At a motel on the Strip, the driver carried her bag into her quarters and left her.

She found herself in a big living room with soft sand-colored carpeting that covered the entire floor. A chartreuse divan matched an overstuffed chair and thick drapes. A radio was playing softly.

She opened a door and found a small but exquisitely furnished bedroom. While she was unpacking her bag, a bellboy brought a pitcher of ice. She tipped him. His appearance reminded her that a guest was coming.

She could not help a feeling of power at having talked Kenney out of his mad scheme to fly to Cuba. Kenney was no weakling—but apparently, she could control him.

Harry Ransome was an even stronger man. Could she get Harry Ransome to do exactly as she wanted?

Melody took a leisurely shower. Naked and peaceful, she studied her reflection in the full-length mirror. She could see changes. Her breasts seemed fuller now, as though they had ripened into maturity.

She dried and powdered her body, gliding the puff almost sensuously over her thighs and stomach, patting and daubing at her creamy flesh. She put perfume behind her ears. The door buzzer sounded.

She slipped on a negligee, hastily buttoning the flimsy white fabric over her ivory breasts and thighs. She would have to make Kenney understand that he had to leave her alone until Sunday afternoon, when they would fly back to California. She opened the door.

The man whistled and muttered, "Wow." He was not Kenney Ward.

She quickly closed the door on him, trying to still the thumping of her heart.

The man outside tapped on the door. "I'm Frank Olney," he said.

"I—I thought you were someone else."

"I presumed as much. May I come in?"

"Now?"

"Well, Harry Ransome gave me to understand I'd be

very welcome here."

Even Harry Ransome's name had a hypnotic effect on her. Had she daydreamed of controlling Harry?

She opened the door again and stood back shyly.

An athletic-looking man of thirty or so came into the room. He wore gray slacks, a plaid jacket and a detached air of assurance. "I'd figured a night on the town before this," he said, "but after seeing you I can't wait."

"You—you can't wait?"

He stared at her, wrinkling his forehead. "You are the girl Harry Ransome told me to meet?"

She nodded wordlessly.

"Then what the dickens are we waiting for?" He took off his coat and tossed it on the divan and began unknotting his tie.

"What are you doing?" she asked.

"I'm undressing, as you can see."

Sudden tears filled her eyes and she fled to the bedroom. She leaned against the closed door trying to stifle her sobs.

Frank Olney tapped on the door. "What gives, baby doll?"

"Is that all you want to do?" She could not cope with this situation. She had not expected this. She realized she had not known what to expect, really.

"My God. Harry told me anything went. Didn't he tell you, didn't he say what you should do?"

Did Harry want her to crawl into bed with a man she had met only minutes before, like a common whore?

"I didn't understand," she protested.

"For the love of pete." Exasperation tinged Olney's every word. "I'm going to call that guy and tell him I've been jobbed."

Melody stopped crying and dried her eyes. What would Harry think? More important, what would he do? Would he take away her pleasant life in California? She could not let Olney call Harry Ransome and report that Melody had failed. She said, "Don't do that, please. I'll be all right now, I think."

"You think? Don't you know?"

She opened the door, looked up at him and smiled. "Yes, I know. It's all right now."

He grinned at her. "That's more like it, baby doll." His muscular arms wrapped tightly about her and she could feel the hammering of his heart. His lips fastened hungrily on her mouth. The man made no pretense of finesse, of love play.

He swept her up and carried her to the bed. The negligee came open. She closed her eyes as his body covered hers. His hands dug into her sides, making her whimper with pain. She endured his frightening passion.

His breathing calmed and she thought he had fallen asleep. But he came alive again when she moved, and he took her again, recklessly and with violence. He lay beside her, never loosening his arms, alternately resting and waking to erotic activity until she felt shamed and degraded. Finally, in the small hours of morning, he fell into exhausted sleep.

THIRTEEN

Melody was quiet on the flight back to California. She begged Kenney to let her go right home when they arrived at the airport. He seemed hurt, but did not insist on her staying with him.

She had a lot of thinking to do.

In the first place, she had been a fool to think she could handle Ransome. A worse fool to sign up for a business course. Ransome was not interested in her secretarial skills. He was not even jealous of her—he did not value her enough to be jealous. He did not mind her pleasing one of his friends.

Would there be a recurrence of what had happened at the motel in Las Vegas? Did Ransome plan to use Melody as a high-priced whore?

She felt trapped and miserable. How could she ever submit again to a beast like Frank Olney who apparently had not had a woman in years, the way he had acted with her? The man had been absolutely insatiable. Her body still felt bruised.

And poor Kenney. He must have expected some reward for giving up his wild plan of flying out of the country. But she had been unable to stand the thought of relations even with a man she loved after her night with Frank Olney.

She felt tears welling up. She seemed to be learning a lot, at any rate, about tears.

To make matters worse, Anita was bubbling with curiosity about the trip to Las Vegas.

"Tell me everything, Melody. Did you have fun? Did you win any money?"

"Sure it was fun." Some fun, she thought. What could she tell Anita if the questioning did not stop?

"Did you see Dean Martin? He's playing in Vegas now. What hotel did you stay in? Where did you gamble?"

"To tell the truth, I didn't do much of anything."

"What do you mean?" Anita asked slowly.

"Well, I got sorta sick. I spent most of the time in bed." At least that part of it was the truth—horribly the truth.

"Oh, you poor dear." Anita put an arm around Melody and kissed her cheek. "I hope you're feeling better now." She led Melody to bed, fussily insisted on tucking her in. "I'll make a cup of warm milk. A good night's sleep and you'll feel like new." She went off to the kitchen while Melody obediently nestled between covers. The feeling that someone cared was a comforting one.

Anita came back with the warm milk. After draining the cup Melody felt better than she had before. Anita sat on the bed and held her hand. She talked inconsequentially until Melody fell asleep.

The days merged into weeks. Melody attended dramatic class on Tuesday and Thursday, dancing Wednesday and Friday. On Saturday she would swim in the pool at the apartment all morning and walk on the boulevard in the afternoon. She slept late on Sunday and Monday was free.

She still attended classes at the secretarial school where her progress was rapid. Ralph Dana tried halfheartedly to resume their friendship—but she put him off and he was not insistent. Her skill in evasive tactics was growing. Even Anita had made no further amative advances.

Melody had several short letters from Kenney in which he spoke mostly about the dusting jobs he had done, and the money he was making. He always signed his letter "With Love, Kenney," and that was the only mention of love in his letters.

One Wednesday afternoon she left the dance studio to find the Matthews Cadillac at the curb with Tony standing beside it, and Linda Matthews in the rear. Melody was puzzled. She usually traveled to and from her lessons by the city bus. Her first half-angry thought was that Linda was trailing her, checking up.

Melody got into the car. They moved into traffic. Linda Matthews took Melody's hand. She said, "Your mother is ill." Melody stared. Effie was always ill.

"She may pull through," Linda continued uncertainly. Melody saw her own overnight bag on the floor of the Cadillac. Mrs. Matthews expected Melody to go to her mother as any normal person would do. Fly to a dying mother's side—that was expected of people.

Melody felt numb. With effort she managed to say,

"I'll have to go, I'll have to go."

"Yes, dear, of course. Anita packed your bag. Mr. Ransome's plane will be at the airport by the time we are. We got the call shortly after you left this morning. After talking to Mr. Ransome I felt we could gain nothing by telling you immediately. We decided you could have your lesson and by that time the company plane would be here."

"Everyone is very thoughtful," Melody said.

She sat upright, her thoughts detached, on the ride to the airport. Mrs. Matthews saw her through the waiting room and out to the ramp. The Ransome plane was parked beyond an airliner. Kenney was coming toward them. Melody had an impulse to run to him, but a curious numbness stopped her.

"I just shut down one engine," he said. "We'd better take off now while we have clearance."

Mrs. Matthews kissed Melody's cheek and stood watching as Kenney and Melody walked to the plane together.

Inside the plane, Kenney gave Melody a quick fierce kiss, then turned his attention to getting them airborne.

On course and running smoothly, he turned to her again, taking her in his arms.

She responded hungrily.

"You should have left there long ago," he said. "That's no life for you, in California."

"Have I a life somewhere else? Would my staying with Ma have solved anything? Nothing at all. She never listened to me."

"I'll buy that. But you and I—we could have a good life together."

"Don't talk about that," she said sharply.

"Okay," he said. "I won't mention it again."

"Don't be angry with me," she begged.

He lit a cigarette. "Listen, kid, I've been angry practically every minute since I got to love you. Not only angry but also a little bit nuts."

"Kenney, don't you want me a little smarter than I was when you first met me?"

"No, damn it, I'd like you just exactly as you were the day I met you."

"I was a country girl—in spades."

"Okay. I wanted you that way."

"You would have tired of me so quickly."

He put a rough finger under her chin and lifted her head. "Look, Melody, baby, all that stuff you're so wild about is superficial. The real you is what I fell in love with, not a clothes dummy, not a cooch dancer. I think those California fruit cakes are spoiling you."

"What do you mean by that last bit?"

"California is full of queer people. Take that roommate of yours, Anita whats-her-name. I'll bet she's queer."

"Anita is a nice girl."

"Is she? She hasn't so many girl curves and she cuts her hair short and always wears slacks."

"That doesn't make her queer."

"No, but I'll bet—oh, hell, I'm saying the wrong

things at a time like this. I'm sorry about your mother."

"Would you think I was awful if I told you I feel nothing? Absolutely nothing?"

"You'll feel it later. Right now, you're stunned, in a way."

She squeezed his brown hand, feeling an affection for him that went beyond love. "Ma never had much joy out of me, I guess. We always moved with the harvest and I guess it was tough on her having a little kid to drag along."

"My guess is she didn't care. I'm surprised you turned out to be the girl you are, Melody. You're so terrific in every way."

His praise made her feel guilty. If he only knew what she had done he would feel differently. She was glad he did not know and she resolved fiercely that he would never find out.

As he prepared to let down and land she wondered what was in store for her. What did she really want of life? A role as wife to a crop-dusting pilot? As much as she loved him she was not ready for any final answer.

Somehow she knew she was not through growing up.

No matter what she told people, she still was just seventeen.

She asked, "Has my mother asked for me, Kenney?"

"I wouldn't know. They've had her in the hospital nearly a week."

The fact that her mother was ill, very seriously ill, was coming through to Melody at last. "Someone should have told me sooner," she said.

She thought of the nothingness that was Effie's life, the succession of worthless men ... And the worthless daughter?

She cried softly and Kenney let her cry.

FOURTEEN

Kenney helped Melody out of the plane. She looked toward the big Ransome house but saw no sign that anyone was home.

"I'll drive you over in the jeep," Kenney said, taking her blue overnight case.

He started the jeep engine and they moved away from the air strip, toward town.

The county hospital was a long low building of concrete block. Kenney, leaving Melody at the entrance, explained, "The boss told me to check you in the motel. I'll run your things over there and then come back."

She thanked him, entered the hospital. The air-conditioning was not working well and the heat in the building was almost unbearable. Melody introduced herself at the desk.

The nurse on duty said, "Your mother's doctor wants to see you, Miss Frane. I'll have him paged. Will you please be seated?"

Melody waited on a couch slip-covered in plastic. A dark-haired Mexican in dirty jeans sat at the other end.

After a few minutes a small chubby man in a white coat walked up to her.

"I'm Dr. Waller," he said. "I've been attending your mother."

"How is she?" Melody said.

"She died just ten minutes ago," the doctor said brusquely. "I'm sorry, Miss Frane."

I'm alone, Melody thought. But I was always alone. Poor Effie—she's alone now, too. She doesn't even have Joe Priddy now.

She realized that the doctor was still talking.

"To be brutally frank, Miss Frane, she drank herself to death. My diagnosis was acute alcoholism. Literally she was still a young woman—but her kind of drinking makes the clock tick faster."

Melody was silent, thinking of the old days, before Effie's looks were ruined. Long ago. The road, the endless road. The lettuce crop, the potato crop—and only once, a man who played a guitar.

The doctor was waiting for her to say something. She spoke mechanically. "Thank you for doing what you could."

He inclined his head and then moved silently away.

She sat on the couch again. She was there when Kenney returned and sat beside her.

"Well, how is she?" he asked.

"She's dead," Melody said and suddenly her throat choked up and she turned to Kenney and he held her close, his hand stroking her back. Her tears came to an end. She wiped her eyes.

"What am I supposed to do?" she asked.

"I'll take you to the motel. You shower and rest. I'll take care of everything."

Kenney was as good as his word. He did take care of everything. That afternoon he drove her to the funeral parlor. Surrounded by soft music and soft lights, Melody's mother lay peacefully in the casket, the dissipated look faded from her face. There was a short service, attended only by Melody and Kenney. Then there was the drive to the cemetery and Effie's role in life was over.

Melody felt drained, even of grief. Kenney drove her back to the motel and left her.

Someone tapped on her door. Melody fought exhaustion, awoke and opened the door. Her visitor was Harry Ransome. He was dressed in the familiar checked shirt, stiffly starched khaki trousers and scuffed boots. He thumbed his cattleman's hat to the back of his head and lounged into the room.

"Sorry about your mother, Melody," he said. "Sad, but considering her condition, it's just as well."

"Just as well?" she echoed.

He lowered himself into the divan and patted the seat beside him.

She seated herself and waited.

"I'm driving over to Phoenix and want you to come along," Ransome said.

"Right now?"

"Just as soon as you're dressed. I'll tell you what's on my mind while we're on the way."

"All right," she said. She started to rise. He reached out a quick hand and pulled her back. He kissed her mouth, then said, "You're getting lovelier every day, Melody."

She looked at him numbly. "Harry, when am I going to work?"

"Work? You're working for me all the time, Melody."

"I mean real work. I was supposed to take your secretary's place, remember?"

He scowled. "You're getting your salary regularly, aren't you?"

"I'd like to feel that I'm earning it."

"Earn it? Frank Olney's working for me, Melody. You accomplished that."

"I did?" Odd. She had not once mentioned to Olney that he might like working for Ransome. He had kept her too busy to say anything.

"You did, yes. That was a stroke of luck for me. I was trying to do some missile work in my electronic plant in Tucson before I got Olney. Now they're trying to do business with me. That's all your doing Melody."

She stopped trying to understand. "I'll get ready," she said. "How long will we be in Phoenix?"

"Just till tomorrow. Better pack something to sleep in, though."

She packed her overnight case hastily. Harry's rust red sports car waited outside.

On the lonely highway he sent the speedometer up

to seventy-five. He could be good company. He told stories about people and places far removed from Melody's world. Occasionally she found herself talking about her mother, recalling long-buried memories. At these times, he listened sympathetically.

They were almost to Phoenix before Harry mentioned the object of their trip. "There's another job I'd like you to do for me."

"Like—like the last one?" she asked. "That was horrible, Harry."

"Listen, Melody. I'm expanding my operations considerably and need a plant down on the coast. Harvey Mattern owns just exactly the set-up I need. His plant is located in Compton. As it happens, he's about to go broke but he's a stubborn man and won't sell or merge."

"But—but, Harry—"

"What's the matter? Aren't I treating you right, Melody?"

"Yes, but this—"

"You know something, Melody? All we get in this world we have to get by doing some things we don't like. That is if we're to be anything but wage slaves. Now me, I'm trying to do Mattern a favor and he won't listen to reason. After this is all over he'll be better off for it, just as Olney is happier working for me than he'd be anywhere else. Most people don't know what's good for them and they have to be urged along."

"I don't feel right about it," she said in a low voice.

"Oh, come off it, Melody. This isn't going to hurt you

in the least. I know a dozen women who'd jump at the chance you've had."

"I do appreciate what you've done. It's not that I'm ungrateful—"

"Then it's all settled. I've reserved a hotel room for you and I'll drive you there. Then I'll get in touch with you later."

The hotel he had named was not the best in Phoenix, but was adequate. Melody was shown to a room on the seventh floor. Somehow her loneliness was immense. She dropped herself on the big bed in the bedroom of her two-room suite and cried for a time.

At a little after midnight she phoned the desk and had a sandwich and glass of milk sent up. She finished eating and room service removed the dishes. She dressed for bed but walked restlessly around the room and then turned on the television set and watched an old movie. What had she become? Where was she drifting? At two she hopefully decided that Harvey Mattern would not show up. There was a tap on her door.

She opened it to find Harry Ransome supporting a big, paunchy white-haired man. "Help me get him in the bedroom," Harry snapped. "The s.o.b. passed out on me."

Together they got the huge-framed Mattern across the room and onto the bed. Ransome straightened, wincing, and mopped his face.

"Now lie down next to him," Harry ordered. "And stay there."

She protested—but Harry started to look enraged, and she did as he said.

She felt her cheeks burning. Harry had left the room. She lay there, rigid, beside a fat balding man in a drunken stupor, wondering if Ransome had gone out of his mind. Occasionally Mattern moved uneasily in his stupor and muttered a few unintelligible words.

After what seemed an eternity, Ransome came back to the room. He motioned her to follow him into the living room.

He grinned. "Now that didn't hurt a bit, did it?" he asked.

"It didn't make sense."

"You did fine, just fine, Melody." He put his arms around her. "I hated to do that, but it was something that had to be done."

"If you'd just tell me why," she said.

"Let's just say that you've done a fine job. And now if you'll just step down the hall to my room, we'll get on with the really important business."

She seemed, as always with Ransome, to have lost all will of her own.

She followed him down the hallway to his room. He poured a stiff drink and offered it to her.

She tried to decline. "I don't like liquor," she said.

He drank the shot himself with one gulp. "Come here to me, baby," he said.

She obeyed. His lips nibbled at her ears and her neck, and then he sat on the divan and pulled her to his lap. "You're beautiful," he said. "The most beautiful thing I've even seen in my life. I could—could eat you, Melody."

"Don't make love to me," she whispered. "My mother —I just buried my mother."

He laughed, picked her up in his arms and carried her to his bed. She closed her eyes and wondered if this was what she had bargained for—this degradation. Kenney had warned her. He had told her she could expect some pretty dismal results if she went along with Ransome's plans. Secretary. As Ransome's body touched hers, she stopped thinking. He possessed her with an almost demented violence. She cried out as his brutal embraces shook her body.

The attack, mercifully short, left her exhausted.

She heard him get up and move around. He came back to the bed with a water glass half-full of whiskey. "Here," he said in a hard voice. "Drink up."

"I don't want to."

"Go ahead," he grated. "Drink it or I'll pour it down your throat."

Frightened, she took the glass. She tasted the whiskey and made a wry face. "Really, I don't want it, Harry."

"Damn it to hell, I said drink it."

She took one look at his face and drained the glass. He took away the glass and lay beside her again. The drink hit her suddenly. She felt dizzy at first and then exhilaration took over. She felt the wild abandon of hatred. She turned and fitted her body against Ransome's, wanting to use him as he had just used her. She sank her teeth in his arm, heard his stifled gasp of pain. His hands tore at her hair. His mouth was fastened on hers. In her strange excited state, she responded wildly, reveling in the onslaught of his passion, assaulting him ...

FIFTEEN

With a sense of being drawn swiftly upward at a dizzying pace, Melody awoke from a black dreamless sleep.

By degrees, her eyes flickered open and she looked about the room without stirring. Her tongue felt fuzzy and her mouth dry. Her head throbbed with an enormous ache. She was sick to her stomach. She groaned and closed her eyes again.

She became aware of sounds—traffic in the street below, people going about their business. She gradually remembered where she was—Ransome's hotel room in Phoenix. Yesterday came back to her in color pictures—driving with Ransome on the desert highway to Phoenix, checking into this hotel, the senseless episode with Harvey Mattern, finishing the night with Ransome. But why this awful feeling of physical illness?

The glass of whisky Ransome had forced her to drink —she had a hangover. She recalled the wild abandon with which she had reciprocated his love. She felt ashamed, and the shame reached through the horrible sickness she felt. She threw off the single sheet that covered her and sat up, only to sink back with a muted groan as the room began whirling. From a prone position she opened her eyes once more. Daylight brightened the room which was empty except for herself.

In the bathroom she drank tap water thirstily. The glass dropped and shattered. She retreated carefully, avoiding the broken shards. Back in the bedroom, she saw the single sheet of paper propped on a chest of drawers. She picked up the sheet of hotel stationery that was covered by Harry Ransome's bold scrawl.

Melody—Had to leave, honey, and didn't want to disturb you. Catch the next plane back to California. I'll see you later. Have fun.

Unsigned. Was that characteristic of Harry Ransome? He would never leave any evidence, she thought, to connect him with a girl and a night in a hotel in Phoenix.

She showered under cold water until her skin tingled. She toweled off and put on her nightgown and negligee. She had to return to the room she had signed for, the room where she had her street clothes. She only hoped she could get there without being seen.

She could hear the hum of a vacuum cleaner somewhere down the hall. A cleaning cart stood at the open door just beyond the one she wanted. She went along the hall close to the wall and reached her door just as the elevator stopped at the end of the corridor. She hurried into her suite. The rooms were empty. The only reminder of the night before was the rumpled bed and the imprint of Mattern's burly body. Her blue overnight case was where she had left it.

She put on the suit she had worn on the drive to Phoenix. The suit was slightly rumpled from the car ride but still presentable. She fixed her face, brushed out her hair and picked up the overnight case. In the lobby she arranged an airline reservation. After toast and a glass of orange juice at the hotel coffee shop, she felt much better.

The airport limousine was announced. Melody retrieved her bag and left the cool air conditioning of the hotel for the hot blast without. Up to this point she had considered nothing but her physical misery, the enormous ill-feeling of a hangover. But a shower and food and the resilience of youth were bringing her senses into focus, and her conscience was taking over.

All in all, Melody Frane was depressed about herself. She felt like an inferior kind of human being. She wondered on the way to the airport if she could go on like this. She realized that Harry Ransome would have other jobs for her—jobs far removed from secretarial skills. She wished that she had married Kenney. But suppose she had brought this feeling of guilt into marriage?

At the airport she went through the loading gate,

under a blazing sun. The plane was blessedly cool. She took a window seat and looked out at the busy airport. The pilot and co-pilot, each with a briefcase, came through the gate and headed for the plane. They caught up with the stewardess and exchanged banter with her, their smiles white in their brown faces.

Uncomplicated people, Melody thought, without problems.

She wished that she were someone else, that she could go all the way back to babyhood, and grow up again with real parents, a real home. Maybe through a miracle like that she could become a real person. Right now, she did not feel real at all. She was a pawn, moved here and there by fate.

"Well, well, this is indeed a surprise."

She looked up at the speaker and did not recognize him at first. Then she gave a start of surprise. "Mr. Olney," she said.

He slouched into the seat beside her. "Don't be so formal," he said. "Now that we work for the same company we can drop the formalities. If our past association doesn't entitle us to dispense with it."

She flushed. He was referring, of course, to their night together in Las Vegas. She thought it cruel of him to bring it up.

"That was quite a little party," he continued cheerfully, but with a thin hint of cynicism. "You played a major role in my life, Melody. It is Melody, isn't it?"

"Yes."

"Yes, quite a role. You became the leading lady. And

it's interesting to meet you again. Quite different, that second look, when a man's not completely in the grip of base human needs."

Melody wished he would not talk like that. He was leading up to something unpleasant, she did not quite know what.

"I don't suppose Ransome will let me have his own delicious little tidbit again, now that he has me in his empire."

"I don't know what you're talking about," Melody said.

"Oh, come off it," he said impatiently. "Don't play innocent with me, Melody."

"Innocent?"

"You're coming on fine. Yes, innocent. I suppose you knew nothing about that camera they had in the next room at the motel."

"Camera?" she echoed. "I don't know what you mean."

He looked at her closely. "I almost believe you," he said. "You should see the film some time, Melody. You're quite a talented young woman with great promise."

She felt her face burning. The plane rose. She had a desire to jump, to destroy herself.

"Are you telling me the truth?"

He was grinning ruefully. "So help me."

Hands clasped in her lap, she asked in a low voice, "They—they made pictures of—of us, doing what we were doing?"

"That's right, Melody. Lovely, beautiful black and white pictures that show every tiny little detail as clear as life."

"Why would anyone want to do a thing like that?"

"This 'they' you're talking about is Harry Ransome. That's how he gets what he wants when everything else fails."

"But—but how can he use those pictures?"

"Don't be a child, Melody. Look, I'm married. Number one, I'd do anything to keep my wife from seeing those pictures. Number two, I work in a supersensitive industry. I hold a top secret clearance. If responsible officials had an inkling that I could be blackmailed I'd lose my security clearance. That means the next thing I'd be doing is truck driving or stevedoring. And frankly, I'm lazy as hell and can't stand the thought of working with my hands and muscles."

Blackmail. Kenney had warned her.

She was silent, thinking of all that had happened since that day in the packing shed, when Len Knight had pinched her behind. That pinch, in retrospect, seemed to have set a chain reaction going that led straight to a Phoenix hotel last night and Harvey Mattern.

Now it was clear to her that Ransome had merely wanted to photograph her and Mattern together in bed. The camera must have been hidden. She knew Ransome would use those photographs to gain his end. No doubt he had tried everything else on Mattern and had used Melody as a last resort. She felt sick inside, a sickness not brought on by the liquor Ransome had forced her to drink.

Thinking back, she realized she had made most decisions in her life without many misgivings. If she only had looked ahead, she would have married Kenney. Now she had to think, had to ask herself if she wanted to survive.

Intruding on her thinking was a vision of Harry Ransome, triumphantly overriding all opposition, using whatever means he could to achieve his purposes.

Maybe she had no right to dream of destroying herself. She did not belong to herself. She belonged to Harry Ransome.

SIXTEEN

Outwardly, Melody's life in California resumed where it had left off when she left to bury her mother. Inwardly, she was a different girl. Her experiences had matured her in a manner that Anita noticed.

"Melody, you're growing up," Anita said one night. The two girls sat on Anita's bed chatting about the world of entertainment with which Anita was so closely associated.

"That's the trouble with living," Melody said. "You have to grow up, or else."

"But you've made such a marvelous transition. When you first came here I thought I'd never seen anyone greener, except maybe me. But now you seem sure of yourself, even more than I am. And Emile told me you were developing dramatic talents. He was so enthused about you that I was actually jealous."

"Anyone who pays Emile gets the same response." Anita did not agree. "He thinks you should try Central Casting for a few parts to get your feet wet. Didn't he tell you?"

"The things that man tells me," said Melody, "are wild."

"Does he try to make love to you?"

"You might call it that. He kisses my feet and ankles."

Anita ran her hand over Melody's knee. "I don't blame him," she said, veiling her eyes.

"Why do you say that?"

"You wouldn't understand." She looked at Melody with troubled eyes. "You so-called normal people irritate me beyond endurance," she burst out. "You never understand." She looked as though she were about to cry.

"I'm very fond of you," Melody said. "I'd like to understand. I'd like to hear you explain yourself."

"I'd rather show you. I'd like to make love to you. Why won't you let me?"

This was deep water, Melody thought. She said, "You're a woman. So am I. The idea of being loved by another woman is repulsive to me. I can't help the way I feel," she apologized. "Maybe it's the way I was brought up. I'm sorry, Anita."

Anita sighed. "Our love could have such infinite

variety. I think I could please you more than any man
ever could."

"Please don't talk that way," Melody said.

Anita reached up and snapped off the bed light. Her
hands moved to Melody's breasts. She murmured
endearments.

"Doesn't this make you want something?" Anita
whispered.

"It makes me wish Kenney were here."

"Damn," said Anita. And that ended it.

Emile Frontenac was beside himself. "Look you here,
my beauty," he fairly yelled at Melody. "I, Emile
Frontenac, who have coached the stars, say that you
have it, that you are ready for the camera. And you
tell me you are not interested."

"But, Emile, I don't want to be an actress. I'm not a
star and I never will be." At this stage, she thought,
she could afford no more dreams—or the smashing of
them.

"I have a friend in TV," he said. "He has a part open.
I spoke to him. It is on a nationally televised program,
Melody, and would suit you. I could help you, my dear,
and bring you to perfection when the play is made."

"I'm going back to Arizona," she said calmly. "That's
where I belong. That's where I want to be."

"Arizona," he said in disgust. "A land of heat and
bugs and savages. Those people in Arizona, all they
do is sell land to one another and buy it back again.
They are nuts."

"Not all of them."

"This pilot boy friend—that is why you go back to Arizona?"

"No, that is not why I go back to Arizona," she mimicked him.

He threw up his hands, then turned serious. "I shall miss you, my dear Melody. I have coached many girls but none with your natural beauty and talents. I do not kiss the feet of all my pretty students, my little one."

"Only those who'll let you."

He cursed softly in French and then laughed with her, kneeling at her feet, and looking up at her with soft eyes. She patted his head and found the hair bristly to her touch.

"Goodbye, Emile," she said softly. "You've been very helpful to me. And very kind."

He kissed her hand and rose to his feet. "Au revoir, my beautiful one," he said huskily. "I shall miss you enormously."

Bart Cameron was less flowery. "I got you too late, kid," he said as he rubbed her legs. "If I'd had you when you were six or seven, you'd be another Cyd. But maybe it's better you get back to the boondocks. This town is full enough of broken hearts."

"Hollywood doesn't have a corner on the broken-heart market," she said.

"Only more than its share." He slapped her legs with both hands. "This is the last rubdown from me,

Melody." He grinned. "Maybe we ought to make it a good one."

"This is good enough," she said. She was tired of being wanted.

"Sometimes I think you're made of ice," he said.

"I'm made of the usual materials. But I've had lots of experience in saying no."

"With a body like yours, you would have. You're made for love, Melody, and I'd like to be the one to give it to you."

She made no comment. The rubdown lost impetus.

"I know the routine," he continued. "You're saving it for the guy you marry. He'll be just as happy if you hand out a little along the way."

"Are you this vulgar with all your students?"

"No. Just the ones I like."

She rolled over on her back and pulled the sheet toward her chin. He massaged her feet, using the ball of his thumb on the balls of her feet. Melody sighed. Bart's hands felt good.

She asked, "After you're with beautiful girls day after day, how can one look different to you from another?"

"Sometimes I can't stand those beautiful girls. You've got a freshness, Melody, that's captivating. Not as much as when you first came to me, but it's still there." He stopped grinning and looked at her solemnly. "Don't ever lose it, honey. It's worth more than anything in the world."

"Will you miss me?"

He frowned. "The dames come and the dames go. But you, yes, I'll miss you very much. You were two bright little spots in my everlastingly dull week."

She sat up, holding the sheet to her full breasts. "I'll miss you, too, Bart. Maybe we'll see each other some time again."

"I don't think so," he said diffidently, "but maybe. If you wait until I come to Arizona you'll never see me again. I hate Arizona. I spent a night in jail in Flagstaff once."

"Whatever for?"

"For making a U-turn in the middle of the street and giving some lip to the policeman who called me for it."

"That's no reason to hate the whole state."

He looked at her wistfully. "Gosh, you're the one, the only one, I regret not being able to make it with. You'd be glorious."

She slapped his hand. "Don't talk like that, Bart. You embarrass me."

"I'll bet. Now get dressed and scram out of here. I got another class in ten minutes."

She walked toward the shower and heard him sigh deeply behind her.

The echo of California, she thought, was always a sigh of parting.

She wondered why she was going back to the desert country—she was hardly going home, since she never had known a home. All she knew was the heat of the road, the endless road—and now she was moving on.

SEVENTEEN

Melody's plane landed at the windblown airport on an August afternoon. She was the only passenger to get off. Arizona, she thought, was unpopular in midsummer.

She sat in the stifling heat of the waiting room. Her taxi was coming from town. The cooler had broken down and a sweating station manager was trying desperately to repair it. He was still working on it when the taxi arrived. Funny, she thought. She had never seen this public airport before—Ransome had his private strip, and always before she had flown in Ransome's plane.

Melody told the driver to take her to Ransome's house.

The place looked brilliant under a ruthless sun.

She saw the twin-engine airplane, parked at tie-downs in the open strip. She saw no sign of Kenney. She paid her driver, put her suitcase in the carport and pushed the front doorbell. An eternity seemed to have passed since that night when Ransome took her under his tutelage, and she had last rung this bell.

Sanchez opened the door. He registered recognition and surprise. "Oh, Miss Melody," he exclaimed in his soft Mexican accent. "So happy to see you. But Senor Ransome not expect."

"Is he here?"

"Si, yes. He just return from Tucson an hour ago."

"Is Mrs. Ransome here, Sanchez?"

The small man looked thoughtful. "No. Senora Ransome is in Santa Barbara for summer."

"Good. Tell Mr. Ransome I'd like to see him."

"He is showering. You wait in study, please."

She waited in the pleasant study, sitting on the intricately tooled leather couch. Her eye traced the design in a Navajo rug on the tiled floor. She wondered about the people who had woven the rug, envying them their art. If you had a skill, she thought, you were a person.

What kind of person was Melody? Was this the life she was meant to lead? Waiting for Harry Ransome to tell her who she was, where and in what capacity she fitted his schemes? She felt she deserved something better.

She moved toward the doors that opened onto the patio. Not too long ago her mother and Joe Priddy had been out there with tall cold drinks, telling Ransome he was in trouble. What a joke. Now her mother was gone. She wondered about Joe Priddy.

She heard a sound and turned.

"I couldn't believe it when Sanchez told me you were here," Harry Ransome said unsmilingly. "Why did you come back, Melody?"

"I had to see you."

"You shouldn't have come," he said. "There was nothing you couldn't handle by telephone, was there?"

"I couldn't handle this by telephone," she said.

He leaned down to kiss her but she avoided his touch. He shrugged, and went to the couch. "All right," he said. "You're here. What's it all about?"

She was close to tears. Life lately had had more than its share of tears. "I want you to marry me," she said.

His eyes rounded for a moment. Then he laughed. "Much as I'd like to oblige you—I already have a wife."

"You don't love her," Melody said. "And she doesn't love you."

He grimaced. "Right on both counts. But I can't do anything about that. I'm stuck with her."

"There's such a thing as divorce."

"Not for me there isn't."

"You can do anything," she said. "I know that, Harry. You can do anything you want to do."

"I wish you were right," he said slowly. "Getting a divorce is one thing I can't do."

"Why not?"

He grinned wryly. "You know how I operate, Melody. If I can persuade a man, I'll persuade him. If he can't be persuaded, sometimes I can buy him. If I can't persuade him or buy him, I get something on him. Then he's mine."

"What's that to do with getting a divorce?"

"Let's say my wife has something on me. If I tried to divorce her—" He broke off, put his hands out in a gesture of appeal. "It just can't be done."

"Then give me the job you promised," she said desperately. "You said you were grooming me for Josie's job. She was your private secretary, wasn't she?"

He walked to the liquor cabinet and poured himself a drink. "I'd like to, Melody," he said slowly, "but the fact is, you just aren't ready for the job. If you'd remained in California, in due time you'd have been ready. I was willing to pay your salary while you learned—"

"I am ready," Melody said. "I went to night school all the time I was down there. I took shorthand and typing and I know office work. Just dictate a letter and I'll show you."

"That won't be necessary," he said testily. He gulped his drink. "I don't like people to make decisions without consulting me. Not when their salary comes from me."

"That means you won't give me decent work?" she asked.

"I didn't say that. I merely expressed my displeasure at your showing up here at the ranch when you should be in California."

"I don't like being a whore," she said.

"Whoa, there. That's your term, not mine. What gave you that idea?"

"Worse than a whore. I met Frank Olney on the plane when I flew back from Phoenix. He told me about the pictures."

"What pictures?"

"You know what pictures, Harry," she said. "Did Mattern turn his plant in Compton over to you?"

"He reconsidered," Ransome said reluctantly.

"How could you do this to me, Harry?" she asked. "I

don't think I deserve it."

"Didn't you enjoy the plush life in California?"

"Not enough to make up for what you did to me."

He poured himself another drink. He raised it to his lips before he spoke. Then he said, "You went into this with your eyes open, Melody. Now you're trying to crawl out."

"I'm not crawling. I'm just asking you to change things."

He seemed to make a quick decision. He said, "You go on to the motel. I'll think about it and see you tonight. Okay?"

She studied him for a long moment. She said, "Okay, Harry."

"I'll have Sanchez drive you to the motel."

"Don't bother," she said. "I want to see Kenney. He'll drive me there."

"Just as you say, dear," Ransome said genially.

She looked at him mistrustfully and left.

When Melody was gone, Ransome lifted the telephone. He reached Oscar Land, his foreman.

"Oscar, you seen that crud Joe Priddy around lately?"

"Boss, last time I seen him was when I give him that twenty a few days ago. You know you told me to keep him happy out of the petty cash and I—"

"Never mind that. Know where you can locate him?"

"He hangs out at a joint down on Santa Fe Street, boss. Place called Dirty Moe's. If he's not there he's probably out at Camp One. I been letting him sleep in one of the cabins out there. You told me to keep him hap—"

"Damn it, I know what I told you. Listen, Oscar, round up Joe Priddy as soon as you can and send him out here."

"Out to your—your house?"

"Yes, to my house. And make it snappy, Oscar. This won't wait."

"You betcha, boss, right away."

Ransome hung up, smiling. That Frane girl needed a damn good lesson to keep her in line. He had an idea that Joe Priddy could teach it—with a little help from some of the ignorant field hands who lacked the get-up to move to the next harvest. They were the lowest scum of all the migratory workers and they suited Ransome's purpose completely.

Ransome poured himself a drink.

Kenney was working on a plane in the shade of the hangar. The craft seemed absurdly small in comparison to the twin-engine one he usually flew for Ransome. The cockpit was open with big hoppers on each side. He swung around when he heard Melody approaching.

A grin spread on his grease-smeared face. He put out his arms. Melody came against him. She felt the beating of his heart.

"Where the dickens did you come from?" he asked.

"I just got tired of everything down there. I wanted to come home—this seems like home, more than any place I've ever been."

He led her to his bench. "Rest there, baby, I'm going to wash up. Back in a jiff."

He returned with face and hands scrubbed clean, coppery hair damp and combed. He sat on the ground at her side and asked wistfully, "Didn't come all the way back here to marry me, did you?"

"Not this trip, Kenney. Still want me?"

He grinned briefly. "Same old me, Melody, still wanting to make you respectable."

They sat close together, unspeaking, Kenney's hand resting on her knee. She put her hand on his. He clasped her fingers. After a long time, she murmured, "Remember the day I had my first airplane ride?"

She leaned forward to see the shape of his face in the waning light, and then she was in his arms. He kissed her fiercely.

"I've missed you," he said.

She felt his caressing hands and his pounding heart as they held one another close—and she knew that she was home. She had no mother, no house here— yet she had flown to Arizona because sanctuary was here, she realized now. The sanctuary of Kenney Ward's arms.

In the shadows they clung closer and closer. He pushed her clothing aside. For a time he was part of her being and her body and she a part of his. They were locked frantically. The only sound was their breathing and the chorus of the night insects.

"Melody?" he asked finally.

"Yes, Kenney."

"You're not going to sleep on me?"

"No," she whispered, kissing his neck. "Don't leave me yet."

"Do you like me?"

She tightened her arms around him. "I love you," she said.

"More?"

"Yes, darling. I want all you've got tonight."

Tonight. This beautiful night. If only this night need never end.

The stars were out when Kenney brought the grill from the hangar and built a bed of coals. He opened a can of beer for himself and a can of cola for Melody. The coals turned red and faded to gray, just right for cooking hamburgers. They ate and then sat silently, sipping their drinks, so close to one another their bodies touched.

Kenney finished his beer and put the can on the ground. "You didn't see my duster before it got dark."

"I saw it. It's beautiful."

He chuckled. "I don't know how a beat-up old duster can be beautiful but it sure is a good little plane. I made seven hundred bucks last week," he told her proudly.

"Kenney—you'll be rich."

"Don't want to be rich, just comfortable."

"What are your plans?"

He spoke slowly. "I don't know—just piling up the money now. Maybe later on I'll have something to do with it. What about you—how come you're back in Arizona?"

"I feel this is my home," she said.

"That's funny. A girl like you who has never had a home, picking a place like this."

"This is where you are, Kenney."

He whispered, "Do you mean that, honey? You came because of me?" He stared at her through the darkness. "This could affect my plans too, you know," he said finally.

"Right now I need sleep," she said, rising. "Will you drive me to the motel?"

He seemed disappointed, but he said, "Sure. You want to go now?"

"Please."

They walked silently to the jeep. Kenney brought Melody's baggage from Ransome's carport.

When they reached the motel, Kenney seemed reluctant to leave Melody for the night. But finally he said, "See you tomorrow."

She held up her face to be kissed and he put his mouth on hers. He turned and went out the door.

She showered and made ready for bed.

She heard footsteps approach and pause at her door. A key turned in the lock.

"Who's there?" she called, anxiously.

The door swung slowly open.

She stared at Joe Priddy's leering, familiar face.

EIGHTEEN

Melody stared, mesmerized by terror. Part of her mind refused to believe in Joe Priddy's reality, in her own vulnerable position. She was fascinated by the wild animal look of him as his gaze roved over her body. That, she thought, is the naked face of lust—the real face hidden behind more civilized ones she had known.

She opened her mouth to scream and he leaped forward and clutched her with one arm. He clapped his evil-smelling hand over her mouth, smothering the cry. He began dragging her toward the door. Someone else came from outside and snapped the lights off. Many hands took hold of Melody in the darkness. There must be three or four she thought. Three or four animals—and me.

Someone squeezed her breast so tightly she moaned. They seemed bent on giving her some kind of punishment.

"Dammit, wait'll we get her away from here," panted Joe Priddy.

"Hell, no, I ain't had a piece since last January. Let's do it right here in the cabin."

"No, hell no," still another voice chimed in, "that damned fly guy might come back."

"Well, pick up her feet, dammit, and let's get out of here."

Someone lifted her feet and Melody felt herself being carried out of the room. The hot night air outside seemed to intensify the feral stink of the men who were abducting her. They hauled her to a dilapidated old car, squeezed her into the back seat. Joe Priddy and another man climbed in front. Melody managed to bite down on the hand that covered her mouth. If she only could scream ... She got a hearty slap that made her head reel.

"That'll teach you, you biting little bitch."

"What'd she do, bite you?" Joe Priddy chuckled. "She always was the spunky one. When I was shackin' with her old lady I used to try and get to her but she wouldn't have none of ol' Joe."

"Guess that pilot's got a better line than you, Joe."

"Or bigger wings," Joe said, laughing gustily.

A groping hand grabbed Melody's breasts, one after the other. A man whistled. "What a pair on this'n."

"She's sure enough stacked," said another. "Who's first?"

"I reckon I am," Joe Priddy said. "Being as how it was me thought it up."

"You thought it up? Well, that's a big laugh, Priddy. I saw Oscar out lookin' for you. And ever'body knows he's Ransome's man. This is Ransome's idea."

Ransome. Melody realized that she was being taken out for a gang rape. Half-crazed with terror and revulsion, she struggled again and earned another blow to the face that made her lose consciousness.

When she struggled up out of the blackness the car

had stopped. The doors were open and someone was dragging her out. Other hands tore at her filmy nightclothes. In the next instant she was on her back in the sand, naked, with one man holding her hands, and another at her feet.

Joe Priddy stood above her. She could hear his hoarse, drink-laced breathing.

One of the men let go of Melody's leg and pushed Priddy aside. "I don't see why you get to go first. Why don't we flip for it?"

"Flip, hell," Priddy growled. "She's mine first. I ain't taking no seconds."

"I think we should flip," the man at Melody's head said in a strained voice.

"Hell, yes, let's flip for first," they all chorused.

"I could of done had her long ago," complained Priddy. "Well, all right. Two of you hang on and we'll odd-man out."

A shape catapulted out of the darkness and a startled yelp came from Priddy before he went down under a crushing blow. The man standing next to him was dropped by another blow. There were cries, more animal than human, as the would-be attackers fled Melody's enraged rescuer. He was Kenney.

Kenney scooped her up in his arms and ran. He stumbled once and she clutched him. He regained his footing and plunged on. She was aware of being shoved into the jeep.

From the rear of the jeep, Kenney produced a work-stained old shirt and a pair of khaki trousers, cut off at the knees. He gave them to Melody and told her to put them on. She slipped into his oversize clothing and came against him and cried quietly and terribly for a long time.

He let her cry and then kissed her and turned on the dashboard lights.

"Outside of a black eye, I guess you're all right," he said shakily.

"How did you happen to find me?"

"I came back to the motel. I wanted to ask you one more time to marry me. I got there just as they were driving away."

"I was lucky," she said simply.

"Whose idea was this party, Melody? Joe didn't dream it up himself."

She was silent.

He continued, "Harry Ransome has to be behind what just happened. This is his kind of deal. He likes to degrade people—trap them—get something on them—and they become his slaves."

She lied, "I don't know who thought this up, Kenney. If Ransome did—then what?"

"I'll fix him," Kenney said wildly. And she was glad she had lied. What would happen to Kenney if he tangled with a powerful man like Harry Ransome— especially if he attacked without plan, in hot anger?

The jeep hit the highway.

"Where are we going?" she asked fearfully.

"To Ransome's. We'll have this out here and now."

And Ransome would destroy him. Kenney had to be

saved from himself, whether Melody were avenged or not. She thought of a desperate expedient. She had never dared tell him the full truth about herself. Now was the time to tell him. "Kenney," she cried, "I'm not worth it. I asked for everything I got. Listen to me—"

"Shut up, sweetheart," he ordered. "Don't say another word. You're afraid of my tangling with Ransome, aren't you? Don't try to stop me, because I can't be stopped."

She wailed softly, "Remember I told you that you were the first? You weren't, Kenney. There was someone else—years back. When I was eleven. A field hand, somewhere in Texas. Ma and I were working the cotton crop then. And this—well, he got me alone and forced me. After that, I was careful about being alone. But he was the first, Kenney—"

The jeep gathered speed. "I believe you," Kenney said. "And after I'm through with Ransome, I'll get this other guy's name out of you, and I'll look him up and settle with him, too."

"Kenney, don't you understand? All right—that time when I was a kid, that wasn't my fault. But later— you know who else was ahead of you?"

"Yes. Harry Ransome. That bragging bastard always said so. One more reason to get rid of him."

"There were men after I went to California. Lots of men. Men Harry introduced me to. I'm no good, Kenney—"

"There were no men in California. You're lying. You're saying that to keep me out of a fight. I've got news for you. You'll have to think up a bigger whopper than that. You're a swell, decent kid, and if a couple of stinkers took advantage of you once, it'll be their hard luck—not yours or mine."

She could have wept and laughed at once. She had been terrified of the moment when she must reveal the truth to Kenney about herself—and now when she wanted him to think the worst of her, he refused to believe anything but good.

She remembered that she had handled him once before in an almost similar moment of madness, when he had been angry enough at Ransome to try to abduct her and fly to Cuba.

She could handle him again.

"I feel sick," she whispered, which was not a lie. "Please, Kenney—before we do anything else—take me some place where I can rest a while."

The jeep slowed, not a great deal, but enough to indicate that some frenzy had abated in its driver "I must be nuts," Kenney stated with awe. "Not thinking of you first. Do you need a doctor, Melody?"

"No, I'd have to talk to a doctor—and I don't feel like talking. Just take me some place where we can be together. And tell me you love me—over and over. Because I love you, Kenney. I wish the whole world was different. I wish I'd met you long ago—before I was eleven."

He said slowly, "That's what I was waiting for. That's the answer I wanted. Know what you sound like, Melody?"

She did not answer.

"You sound," he replied for her, "Like a girl who's ready to get married."

"I guess I'm ready now," she admitted in a small voice. "If you still want me, Kenney. I guess I'll never want to stay alone again at night the rest of my life."

The jeep pulled to the side of the road and stopped.

He took her in his arms. Shakily he said, "This is crazy. We could go anywhere in the world—I'm the guy with wings, remember? We could use my good little duster and fly to Acapulco and rent the best suite in the city. We'd get married right there in Mexico, as legal as anywhere else. It's a gorgeous dream, isn't it, baby? But what I want right now is just to smooch with my girl in a parked jeep in the dark—"

She came into his arms with a hurt little sob that was half-joy and half-fear. She whispered his name and stroked his cheek. The night about them was dark and vast—but the vastness, she thought, was only Kenney's back yard. Wherever the air could support a pair of wings, by night or day, she would be safe with Kenney. With him, the night had no bad dreams.

His hard demanding mouth caressed her with a new tenderness. His voice had an almost crooning note. "My girl. My Melody."

She cradled his head in her arms while his mouth and hands explored her hungrily. She felt a tenderness that equaled his, and was surprised by the feeling— she had not felt this for her mother and there had been no one else who was related to her. "We're each other's family now," she murmured.

In their dark corner to the quiet world, they did not know another car passed occasionally on the highway. They did not hear the jetliner four miles above them, bound for the east where the sun would be born again. They were alone in the universe, a woman and a man.

This was the moment, Melody thought, in which she really became a woman. As their bodies meshed in the awkward space, as they laughed at the awkwardness and accommodated themselves to it, she felt as though this were truly the first time for her—the difference was beyond measure—as though not even she and Kenney had been lovers before.

The difference must come from her promise to marry him. Now she knew beyond doubt that there would never be anyone else. No Harry Ransome. No Frank Olney, No one ever as long as she lived, to fondle and arouse her, to inflame her desire and not satisfy it.

She wanted to please him. She had always been glad she had a beautiful body because her body had been her asset, something to trade with life for a better set of circumstances than the miserable ones she had been born to. Tonight she was glad of her beautiful body for another reason. Poor as she was, she had a wonderful gift for the man she loved—herself. A gift, she thought, which could be given over and over, and of which, if she was lucky, he would never grow tired.

She became aggressive in her joy. Her hands explored his maleness, her lips made gentle little plays at his throat.

He moaned with longing.

They held one another, shuddering, making love with more than their bodies, breast to breast, thigh to thigh, thoughts no less muted.

NINETEEN

After a long while eternity dwindled back to this one night and then to this one moment in a jeep parked by the highway.

They came back together.

Melody said with a whisper of laughter, "After we have children we'll never be able to tell them we did a crazy beautiful thing like this—they won't believe it."

His answering voice was urgent, excited. "I still want to fly to Mexico—even if it's just for a few days. In fact, I think it's one of the best ideas I ever had in my life. We'll get married down there, spend a million bucks on the time of our lives and come back and make another million. With you rooting for me, Melody, I'll be a bigger man than Harry Ransome ever pretended to be. Watch and see."

Even the sound of Harry Ransome's name had become hurtful to her, an ugliness in itself. "Don't speak of him," she begged. "I'd like to forget that I ever knew him. Let's go back to my motel and get my things—and then we'll do anything you say. If you say Mexico, so do I."

He hugged her affectionately. The touch seemed to arouse her once more and she put her hands on his cheeks and pulled his face to hers for a kiss. His answering kiss turned from a cheerful casual one to something longer—

Suddenly he pushed her away. "Watch it, woman," he warned her not quite steadily. "We might spend the rest of our lives right here if we don't get a move on. Easiest thing in the world—just kissing and making love." He released the brake.

She cuddled beside him on the high hard seat, feeling as though his work-stained shirt and castoff pants were the most glamorous clothes she had ever worn. They had covered her shame at first—now her shame was wiped out. Kenney's love had done that for her.

They drove toward the motel where, an eternity ago it seemed, she had expected to spend a quiet night's rest.

She knew something was wrong when she saw that her cabin still was lighted. She was almost sure the place had been dark when Joe Priddy and his gang had dragged her out of there. A word crossed her thinking, scaring her, because it suggested the unknown. Police—maybe one of the would-be rapists had been picked up because he looked suspicious. Maybe he had confessed and now she would have to get involved with his punishment—she had no time to punish or get even with anybody.

She needed all the rest of her life for being in love with Kenney Ward. Could she make people understand that?

The cabin had an occupant, all right. Not one she had expected, although when she saw him she was not particularly surprised.

Harry Ransome.

He had been moving about nervously, she realized, pacing the floor, leaving half-burned cigarette butts in every ashtray. Harry, in starched khaki pants and checked shirt, the lord and master of this part of the world, suddenly looked like a small man and a frightened one.

Joe Priddy must have told him that the plan to degrade Melody, to take away her last shred of self-respect and control of her own destiny, had misfired. Harry must have worried—he must always have worried, Melody thought with a certain contempt.

He had never been a strong important man, really —he had just pretended to be strong and important by playing people against each other, tearing them down to something lower than himself or at least as low. He was Mr. Nobody, playing a part—and maybe that was what his wife had on him, in one way or another, which was why he could not divorce her.

Harry stopped pacing as Melody and Kenney entered the cabin.

She had been afraid Kenney would get in trouble by tangling with Harry Ransome.

But now that the two men met, an opposite thing happened from what she had expected.

Kenney, standing behind her so close that they

touched, said slowly to the man whose plane he had piloted, "You poor loused-up devil. You wanted to hurt my girl. You'll never hurt her. You know that now, don't you?"

The man who lost his head, who started hitting, was not Kenney, but Harry. He came at Kenney in an almost laughable way, like a large child having a tantrum.

Kenney grinned. He pushed Harry Ransome off and the push sent the rancher sprawling onto a divan.

"Stay put," Kenney said. "Don't get up till I tell you. Or so help me I'll turn you inside out."

"You can't talk to me that way," Ransome said.

But he did just as Kenney said.

He stayed on the divan, glaring at both of them in fury and growing fear.

"I know why you're here," Melody told him softly. "You wanted to know what the worst thing was that could happen to you—for what you tried to do to me. Now you're afraid I'll tell the whole world about your schemes. You came here to persuade me—isn't that what you told me once?—or to buy me—or to get something on me. You can't persuade me any more. I'm no longer for sale. And all you can get on me is that I once was fool enough to have dealing with you. You can't hurt me without hurting yourself worse."

Ransome seemed to grow calmer. He looked from Melody to Kenney and then back at Melody again. "All right," he said. "So you won't work for me any more—and you got away from Priddy. I admit I sent him after you. What are you going to do about it?"

"Nothing," Kenney said. "We're leaving here tonight. We're not coming back. And what we're doing with you is nothing. What you've done to yourself for years is punishment enough for any man."

Harry came to his feet at last. He moved toward Melody, his face aging as he moved, so that for the first time the face seemed to match his dramatic white hair. "Melody," he begged in a voice that had lost its note of command, "don't go, don't leave me. Listen. I'll give you everything. The hell with my wife—I'll get rid of her, anything you ask. I'll marry you."

Melody stepped backward, at once fascinated and disgusted by the change in Harry Ransome. She could sense Kenney's startlement—he too was astonished at the transformation.

"You're youth," Harry went on. "Youth and life and loveliness—and I'll be old if you leave me. If you stay with me, I'm young and strong. Melody, don't leave me."

"Pay no attention to him," Kenney said in a soft voice, as though Ransome were a troublesome stranger. "Go pack your things—let's get out of here fast."

Ransome turned his appeal to Kenney. "Don't stick yourself with her for the rest of your life," he warned the pilot. "She's all right for me—but you're different, you can't afford a mistake. Let me tell you what she's been. I have pictures. I'll show you. She's been any man's for a price—"

Again Melody was afraid of what Kenney might do to the older man. But Kenney simply said, as much in pity as contempt, "Dreams, Ransome. A lot of bad dreams. The things you want to tell me never happened. The pictures are dreams and fakes. Get out of Melody's way."

Once more the rancher tried. "Aren't you even grateful?" he asked Melody. "What can he give you that I can't give you better?"

Melody knew the answer. Kenney could give her love. She thought of the frustration and restlessness with which Ransome's lovemaking had left her—and realized that he must have communicated only his own restlessness and frustration.

Harry Ransome, the man of a hundred women, the great financier, great lover, great everything, might as well never have had a woman or a dollar, and perhaps others besides Melody had discovered that about him.

He had enjoyed life as little as Melody had enjoyed her early career as an itinerant crop worker. There was something vital missing inside him—the capacity for joy.

And therefore he would never give joy to anyone else.

He could give a girl the world plus a million dollars —and she still would have no pleasure of the gift.

Whereas Kenney—little shivers ran through her just at the memory of those moments a short while ago in the parked jeep. From now on, life would be filled with incredible moments—and hours—

Why try to explain to Ransome? He would never understand. That was part of what was wrong with him. Might as well explain the color of a sunrise to a man born blind.

"I have to go, Mr. Ransome," she said. "Please excuse me." She added with unconscious irony, "Thanks for everything."

She walked past him. In a matter of a minute or so, she had packed everything she wanted and had changed hastily into decent clothes.

"Here I am, Kenney," she greeted the man she loved, as she came out of the bedroom.

She did not even notice that Ransome had gone away, like the bad dreams Kenney had mentioned. She saw only that Kenney was waiting with a smile that was all for her.

THE END

William E. Vance Bibliography
(1911-1986)

Novels:
Hard Rock Rancher (Popular Library, 1953)
The Branded Lawman (Ace, 1952)
Avenger from Nowhere (Ace, 1953)
Way Station West (Ace, 1955)
Apache War Cry (Popular Library, 1955)
Homicide Lost (Graphic, 1956)
Outlaws Welcome (Ace, 1958)
Day of Blood (Monarch, 1961)
The Wolf Slayer (Ace, 1964)
Outlaw Brand (Ace, 1964)
Tracker (Avalon, 1964)
The Wild Riders of Savage Valley (Ace, 1965)
Son of a Desperado (Ace, 1966)
The Raid at Crazyhorse (Ace, 1967)
No Man's Brand (Ace, 1967)
Drifter's Gold (Doubleday, 1979)
Death Stalks the Cheyenne Trail (Doubleday, 1980)
Law and Outlaw (Doubleday, 1982)

As by George Cassidy

Range War West (Phoenix, 1950)
The Flesh Market (Merit, 1961)
Bait (Beacon, 1962)
Sin Circus (Epic, 1962)
Wanton Bride (Bedside, 1962)
Assignment: Seduction (Merit, 1963)

William E. Vance was born June 21, 1911, in Virginia, Alabama. He graduated from Marion Institute and did graduate work at the University of California Berkeley and the University of Utah. He taught creative writing at the University of Alabama and worked for the Federal Aviation Administration in Utah before moving to Seattle in 1968. Vance's short stories first appeared in the early 1950s in magazines like *Argosy* and *Esquire*, before he turned to writing westerns and crime novels. He wrote more than 40 novels over the next 30 years under his own name and that of George Cassidy, including *Hard Rock Rancher, No Man's Brand* and *Drifter's Gold*. Vance died in Seattle, Washington, on May 1, 1986.

BLACK GAT BOOKS offers the best in reprint crime fiction from the 1950s-1970s. New titles appear every month, and each book is sized to 4.25" x 7", just like they used to be. Collect them all.

Stark House Press

1315 H Street, Eureka, CA 95501 (707) 498-3135
griffinskye3@sbcglobal.net www.StarkHousePress.com
Available from your local bookstore or direct from the publisher